IT'S
THE END
OF THE
WORLD
AS WE
KNOW IT

SACI LLOYD

IT'S THE END OF THE WORLD AS WE KNOW IT

h

Hodder
Children's
Books

A division of Hachette Children's Books

First published in Great Britain in 2015
by Hodder Children's Books

A Catalogue record for this book is available from the British Library

Typeset in Berkeley Book by Avon DataSet Ltd,
Bidford-on-Avon, Warwickshire

ISBN 978 1 444 91668 3

Printed and bound in Great Britain by Clays Ltd, St Ives plc

The paper and board used in this book are natural recyclable products
made from wood grown in responsibly managed forests.
The manufacturing processes conform to the environmental
regulations of the country of origin.

Hodder Children's Books
A division of Hachette Children's Books
338 Euston Road, London NW1 3BH
An Hachette UK company

www.hachette.co.uk

For my Anna,
Mother of Dragons!

Q: How many mad scientists does it take to change a light bulb?

A: Two. One to hold the bulb, the other one to turn the universe.

In the beginning ...

Deep, deep underground, in the belly of the Hadron Super Collider on the French-Swiss border on a gloomy Monday morning, Xenon Deva flicked a switch and tore open a rip in the fabric of space and time. As soon as he realised what he'd done, Deva gasped and then threw his head back in a classic Mad Scientist Laugh. He laughed until he was all laughed out and then he squeezed out one last insane hiccup. He'd waited his whole life for this moment!

Before his eyes, the dancing atoms in the rip began to glow a fiery red. Deva raised his fist to his mouth and bit down on the knuckle. It was working perfectly. He was going to be the badass of the world. Genius, entrepreneur, billionaire, founder of the super-secretive DEVA Corporation, Grand Master of the Ever So Slightly Knock-Kneed Order of Californian Futurists and of course, two fries short of a Happy Meal – he was going to

1

change the world forever. The age of stupidity was over. It was time for science to take over.

Deva ran his trembling hand through his hair and unfortunately for him, in this one simple move, he blew his life's work sky high. For, as he ran his fingers across the surface of his scalp, a single follicle broke free from his slicked-back silver mane. The lone hair began to fall but, as it dropped, it was caught by a gentle current of vault air, which carried it, oh so gently, directly into the crackling heart of the rip.

A blinding jag of light exploded across the vault, hurling Deva against the far wall, where he slumped, unconscious, in the corner. Maybe it was a mercy that he wouldn't have to witness the moment his master plan was flamed to a crisp. Maybe it would have driven him mad. Maybe he was already mad to begin with and it would have driven him sane. We'll never know. All we do know is in that instant, reality took a pretty big punch to the guts. For now, instead of one Earth, teeming with seven billion crazed ape descendants, there were suddenly two – the second made in his very kooky image. In the blink of an eye, the universe had gained seven billion parallel Kalifornians. It was not one of the universe's better days.

And so the story you're about to hear is the tale of these two planets. Or more specifically, of how a boy, a shadow sister, an infobot, a megalomaniac synthetic cat, a crew of Imperfectibles, some pirates and a parrot got caught up in some crazy doo-doo together.

1

Up in his bedroom, Mikey Malone grinned a wolfish grin. Things were going good. Really, really good. He'd already completed:

Phase one: *getting Caitlin up into his room.*

And the night was still young. Oh so young. Now it was time to move on to:

Phase two: *persuading Caitlin that he cared.*

Phase two was vital because Caitlin was a girl who *cared* about stuff. She was a girl who last year collected over ten thousand signatures for a Horned Beetle Relocation Project in sub-Saharan Africa – and Mikey knew if he was going to get anywhere with her, he was going to have to come up with some pretty rock-solid evidence of love for his fellow man. This was tricky as Mikey didn't give a rat's arse for his fellow man, but Caitlin was the hottest girl on the block and he was going to give it his best shot. And so he'd come up with a Master Plan.

GERILLR. He was going to pretend to be the online spy's biggest fan, because GERILLR was just the kind of radical guy that girls who cared about stuff cared about.

Mikey rubbed his unruly hair up into a wiry peak, then caught sight of himself in his bedroom mirror and quickly smooshed it down again. For a moment, his comical eyes stared back at him from his mobile face and he raised a quizzical eyebrow at his own reflection before turning to glance nervously at the clock. Only two minutes to go till GERILLR came online.

Keep cool, Malone, this plan is going to work, he crooned to himself, but his nerves twanged like a donkey's gizzard.

And then, from outside, there came a piercing cry.

'IIIDDIIIOOOOTTT!'

Mikey froze. This was impossible! He had personally locked the diabolic owner of the voice in the bathroom half an hour ago.

'BUMHOLE!'

There was a sudden vicious scrape of claws at the window. Mikey whirled round. His eyes locked onto the furious eyes of his nemesis. Ubu the parrot.

'Oh! Awesome!' cried Caitlin, jumping up. 'Is he, like, yours?'

He recoiled. 'No way! He's my aunt's.'

The girl darted over to the window.

'He's gorgeous. Can I let him in?'

And before Mikey could stop her, she flung up the pane and the parrot flew inside, performing a triumphal circuit of the room while singing, 'I BE BA-A-CK BA-Y-BY!' before coming to land on a dusty anglepoise lamp on Mikey's desk.

Caitlin burst out laughing. 'He's so cool!'

Mikey frowned. Ubu wasn't cool. Ubu was a miniature parrot warlord who ruled the house with a claw of iron and who'd hated him on first sight. Mikey would like nothing more than to flush him down the toilet, but his aunt adored the wretched bird and making her angry wasn't an option – especially as this stay looked like it was going to be even longer than usual. His mum was really bad this time.

Mikey clenched his fist in anger. He wasn't going to let Ubu knock him off the Caitlin Master Plan. It had taken him weeks to plan it perfectly. So, deliberately turning his back on the avian menace, Mikey reached for his computer tablet, and then sat casually on his bed. He dropped his voice down an octave.

'Hey, it's nearly time for GERILLR's spycast,' he growled.

Caitlin's attention immediately snapped back to him.

'You're into GERILLR?' she breathed.

'Sure. Been following him for years,' drawled Mikey, his voice so low he could feel his kidneys vibrate.

Feeling the tide turning against him, Ubu launched himself from the lamp and started to circle overhead in a scornful loop.

'LIAR LIAR PANTS ON FI-RE!'

But Mikey was on a roll now. Blocking the bird like an ice-cool pro, he turned the tablet screen towards Caitlin as the page loaded.

'Remember when GERILLR hacked the Pentagon?'

'Totally.' She came and sat next to him on the bed, nodding enthusiastically.

'And what about when he went after that Chinese politician's sex thing?'

'Oh, yeah. Crucial,' Caitlin agreed, eyes shining.

Ubu landed on the headboard and flapped his wings angrily in her face.

'SEX BOMB SEX BOMB YOU MY SEX BOMB!'

But Caitlin was all Mikey's now. She moved even closer, her thigh briefly touching his as she leaned forward to view the screen better.

Mikey mouthed '*loser*' at Ubu before praying a little prayer of thanks to GERILLR. Oh you caring, sharing piece-of-crap mystery online-activist dude . . . Oh you genius, you're gonna get me la-id! No one would ever look down on Mikey Malone again – the kid from out of town with the crazy mum – not after word spread that he'd made out with Caitlin.

On-screen, GERILLR's underground spycast began to load. Mikey tapped his foot impatiently. There was always this cult-like bit at the start of every broadcast where the hacker contacted an online follower and they did this little suck-uppy thing together. Un-be-liev-ably bor-ing. Mikey moulded his features into an expression of avid interest. And then, suddenly, a black rectangle appeared on his tablet screen, blocking half the page.

Mikey frowned. What was this, some advertising BS? Text started to appear in the box.

>HELLO MIKEY . . .

He sucked his teeth. Definitely some dumb marketing thing. He stretched out his forefinger to X it away. And then he stopped.

>IT'S ME, GERILLR. THERE'S SOMETHING REALLY BIG GOING DOWN . . .

'Oh my God,' squealed Caitlin.

Mikey stared at the screen in shock.

She grabbed his arm. 'It's you! He's picked you!'

>I'VE GOT TO TELL YOU QUICK. I'M IN DANGER.

Mikey swallowed. He didn't give a gnat's fart about GERILLR. Caitlin's hands on his body and the smell of her perfume was driving him insane. Red-hot flames shot up and down his body. Her face was centimetres away from his, he could just lean forward and—

'Mikey? You've got to answer him!' Her voice was urgent. 'There's, like, millions online watching . . .'

He nodded like a man in a trance and was stretching out a shaky hand for the keyboard when Ubu suddenly snapped and hurled himself off the bed post, screaming, 'BELL BOY, BELL BOY!' whilst lunging with his razor-sharp beak at Mikey.

Snapping out of his daze, the boy yanked his arm sideways and the tablet slipped from his grasp. Fumbling, he tried to catch it with his other hand, his fingers forming a clumsy fist around the edges. And that's when Mikey felt the pull – a tug so powerful it dragged him to his knees on the bedroom floor. He stared at the tablet in astonishment. The pull had come from inside the device . . . and it still had a fast hold on him, like it was somehow glued to his skin. He couldn't break free. Using all his strength, Mikey pulled the device up to his face, but all that was visible was the glowing golden ape – the GERILLR icon – from between his splayed fingers . . .

'What're you doing?' hissed Caitlin.

'I – I dunno,' he gasped. He jammed his free hand against the floor, trying to get some purchase on the threadbare fabric of the carpet, but it was no good – he was being dragged across the room. Suddenly the walls began to shake. Mikey stared wildly around. What was happening? The shake turned into a heavy tremor. He desperately tried to get up, but it was no use. An invisible force was pinning him down through the tablet. And then the tremor exploded into a drumming roar of sound. The bedroom window shattered, spraying glass across the room.

'What's going on?' screamed Caitlin, desperately shielding her face.

'Get out of here!' shouted Mikey, trying to heave himself towards the hallway, but he was yanked back again, this time with far greater power than before. He slammed into the desk. Twisting his head he saw Caitlin standing in the doorway with a look of pure terror on her face.

'Run and get help!' he cried.

She stood for a second, frozen.

'Go!'

And then Mikey was suddenly aware of wildly flapping wings overhead. Ubu was swooping in for the kill. He stretched up a hand to bat the bird away but just as he touched its wings, a blinding jag of light struck the bedroom wall and exploded across the room – and the last thing Mikey saw before he was ripped away from the best evening of his miserable life was the GERILLR icon.

It blazed for a second, its afterimage stamping itself onto his retina like a dazzling brand.

Everything went black.

And then he landed, hard, on unknown ground and lay like a dead thing, too astonished to even take a breath.

* * *

Somewhere on the edge of the night sky, two little cubes sat side by side, trembling with anticipation, their eyes round as saucers as they watched the rip whip across the starry sky in a shower of glowing sparks.

'Ooooh,' said the first cube.

'Preetttty,' said the second.

'Are you winking thot I'm thinking?' said the first.

The second one nodded. 'Deah, yude.'

The tiny creatures turned, high-fived each other and burst into high-pitched giggles. Then they bent down and, picking up a miniscule surfboard apiece, they jumped onboard and began to paddle into the gentle night air. They knew a rip in the fabric of time and space like this only came up once in a generation. It was time to surf.

2

Deep, deep below Silikon Vallé, Kix Kaloux leaned against the pockmarked wall of a desolate data tunnel, transfixed by the face of a young girl. A soft, dappled light filtered through the swaying branches that arched over the girl's head, giving the landscape a dream-like quality. The girl was running towards her, getting closer with each step.

Kix leaned forward, drinking in her face. Snub nose, a swirl of freckles over her cheeks, eyes full of clear childish happiness. And then suddenly the girl swerved abruptly to the left. Kix didn't have time to dodge out of the way and the girl ran straight through her body. Kix gasped and retreated a few paces down the tunnel – there was no way she was going to break this hologram file after all the years it'd taken her to find it. She turned to focus on the scene again. The little girl was now running up a sweeping driveway that led to a modern park house, set back a little in the trees.

As the child raced up the drive, the front door slid open and a woman appeared. At her face, Kix strained forward, desperate to get a better look, but some palms in the foreground were blocking her view. The woman suddenly called out, and dropping to her knees, she opened her arms wide. Catching sight of her, the girl lifted her head and, covering the remaining distance in a few rapid strides, she leaped, giggling, into her mother's embrace. For a long moment their arms closed around each other in a tight grip of love. In the dark data tunnel, a tear trickled down Kix's cheek, but her eyes never left the two figures for a second.

Suddenly, the tunnel began to vibrate. Kix staggered sideways, desperately trying to keep the hologram steady. And then, out of nowhere, a blinding jag of light ripped through the tunnel. She flung up a hand against the glare, straining to keep the child in sight. But she was gone. As was the woman and the garden, and the house. Kix let out a strangled cry, but it was all she could do to keep her feet. The tunnel walls around her began to shake violently. And then, BOOM! A flow of wild energy surged through the passageway, knocking her sideways. Her forehead smashed against the wall and she fell to the floor. Her vision blurred, began to darken – but before she lost consciousness, she suddenly caught sight of a tiny golden ape that blazed like a brand in the swirling air.

'What's that?' she whispered, but then her eyes fluttered shut and everything went black.

The tunnel fell quiet, apart from a sudden soft click as the glowing Koral around Kix's neck turned from bright pink to a dead grey.

For a long moment, Kix lay motionless on the corroded floor of the tunnel. The energy wave had died away as quickly as it had come, leaving a deep well of silence behind it. And then, after another pause, something rustled. A very little rustle, it was, from a very little something, deep in the folds of Kix's scarf. And then whatever had rustled, sneezed. Then a tiny hand appeared – and then another, followed by a too-big head, a bendy torso and a pair of very elastic legs. No bigger than Kix Kaloux's thumb, the creature shinned up the fabric of the scarf and clambered up behind her ear before tiptoeing out onto her chin. Now he was fully visible you could see he had a slight glow to him, like a radioactive particle in a 50s B-movie. He balanced there, apparently deep in thought as he examined her head, from the acid green tips of her hair, across her camo-toned skin before coming to rest on her full pink lips.

He jammed his hands on his hips.

'Well, cheeze my nachos if the girl izn't out like a light!'

And then, squeezing his eyes shut, he started to shake from the eyebrows down, turning his glow deep red. When he'd got up a decent flame, he jumped a full metre into the air, curving over onto his back on the descent and landing with a body flop on the girl's cheek, in the manner of a very small and very spicy-hot high jumper.

'Ow!'

In a movement too fast for the naked eye, Kix's hand flew up and closed around his body.

'Owwww!' she cried again as his glow burned her palm. Yanking herself upright, she opened her fist and glared at the little creature.

'What are you doing?'

He cocked his head.

'Oi! You izn't dead then?'

Kix rolled her eyes.

'BitZer. You're such a little . . .' she paused, searching for the right word, '. . . Robo*dik*.'

BitZer gazed back at her, calmly. 'Ah, quit moaning, you're tougher than a two-dollar steak. And anywayz, if you'z too cheap to carry a medibot, then me iz what you got.'

Then he grinned and, with a deft backflip, vaulted back into her scarf.

Kix touched her forehead gently and groaned.

'Man, what *was* that? Felt like a bomb or something.'

'Don't know.'

'Some infobot you are.'

BitZer tapped his head. 'I waz focusing on keeping the hologram alive.'

'Is it gone?'

'Totally. Memory filez is alwayz weak, you know that.'

Kix dropped her head in her hands. 'All that work for nothing. Are you sure?'

'Yeh. I'z sorry dude. Looks like all the data in this tunnel is wiped out, too. Mebbe it'z for the best, tho.'

Her eyes flashed. 'No it isn't! One minute with my family is all I got? That ain't right, BitZ!'

He stared back at her, his cobalt-blue eyes unreadable.

Kix rose unsteadily to her feet. 'Come on! I'm going to find out what happened.'

A light suddenly appeared at the far end of the tunnel.

'W-whatz that?' BitZer shrank into a fold of fabric, his glow fading to a dull outline.

Kix rose to her feet.

'Let's go and find out.'

'No wayz!'

She mimed bird wings.

'Chicken.'

BitZer quivered. 'I can't helpz it. I izn't butch like you.'

'I ain't butch, I'm *fierce*.'

BitZer groaned. 'You're dumber than a road lizard iz what you are. Why you alwayz gotta head towardz trouble?'

Kix frowned but, despite herself, a smile tugged at the corners of her mouth.

'Just naturally contrary, I guess,' she whispered, setting off towards the light.

BitZer pursed his little lips, but his glow had already started to fire up again – for a fraction of a second, when the smile caught the girl's eyes, it had captured a glimpse of what few people ever got to see: Kix Kaloux without her guard up. It was a face with vivid things in it, with fiery eyes and a bright passionate mouth – and the smile that had flashed across it made it seem both lovely and sad. Even if a fraction of a second was all BitZer got before her guard slammed down again.

3

A few feet further up the tunnel, Kix froze.

A hideous cackling scream that sounded like a pirate gone mad, and went something like, 'HA HAH HOOO HA HAH HAHAHAHA OOOORGGGGHAHHAHA!' bounced along the tunnel wall towards her.

'What's that?' she whispered.

'Dunnoz,' came a faint whisper from inside her scarf.

'FATTYBUMBUM!' came another shriek.

'It's coming from just beyond that light.'

Kix chewed her lip. Whatever it was, it sounded pretty small. She took a pace forward.

'Hey . . . Hello?'

The passageway suddenly fell silent.

'Hello?' she ventured again.

'UP YER BUM!' came the furious answer.

Suddenly, Kix Kaloux was furious herself. Ripped out of the most precious moment of her life, sworn at by a

19

potty-mouthed invisible idiot, she wanted answers and she wanted them now.

'Up yer own bum!' she shouted, and, raising her optic-nerve light sensors to Hi-Intensiti, she walked to the end of the tunnel and strode around the bend, right into the flight path of Ubu the parrot.

Kix caught sight of a flash of red, and flinging up her arm to protect herself, she lost her balance, tripped and fell on something soft. Heart in mouth, she retreated, flattening herself against the burnt-out wall.

After a few moments, she forced herself to look around. The bird had gone and the soft thing hadn't moved. She gulped some air. This panic wasn't helping her one bit. She needed to rebalance her adrenalin levels. Lifting her forearm, Kix tapped a panel and immediately the hormone levels began to drop. Eventually, she felt calm enough to inch forward. She now saw the thing was not a thing, but a boy. She leaned over him. He was very pale and lay perfectly still, his eyes wide open like a dazed bird that had flown into a window. She waved her hand in front of his face, wondering why his medibots hadn't kicked in. And that's when his smell hit her. She wrinkled her nose.

'Pooh,' she said.

Mikey blinked and opened his eyes.

'Huh?' he said.

Kix wafted her hand in front of her face. 'Pooh-ee!'

Mikey lifted his head, desperately trying to get the figure kneeling over him into some kind of focus. Through the wooze he could make out she was a girl, although the most outlandish looking one he'd ever seen. The left side of her body was covered with what appeared to be snakeskin – a pattern that ran under a semi-translucent bodysuit all the way from her cheekbone down to her ankle. He jerked up on his elbows, wondering if she was real or not.

Pinching her nose, the girl inched away from him.

'I'm sorry, frère, but that's just nasty.'

Mikey stared at her for a long moment, before he was able to make out what she was saying.

'I – I smell?' he stuttered.

Kix tapped her scarf. 'BitZ, come check this out.'

Mikey sniffed the air around him cautiously. Maybe he'd pissed himself and hadn't realised, like those winos round the back of the cash and carry. But his nose came up with nothing. A bit sweaty, maybe . . . but nothing to deserve the kind of lip this girl was giving him. He shook his head, desperately trying to work out how he got from his bedroom to . . . wherever this was. He pulled himself to his knees. Strange shapes seemed to throng about him

21

in the dark tunnel, and a low irritating hum kept his brain from focusing.

'Where am I?'

BitZer's head appeared over the top of Kix's scarf, his eyes widening as he took in the boy.

'Oooh. Strange.'

Kix fanned the air. 'I know. But I seriously doubt this dude knows anything.'

Mikey stared at her. 'Are you talking to me?'

Kix fixed him with her eyes. 'I wasn't. But I am now. Buddy, I know this is a dumb question, but I have to ask. You didn't just cause that big bang back there did you?'

Mikey shook his head eagerly. 'No, I was just going to ask you the same thing. I was in my bedroom at home and the next thing I knew there was a massive explosion and I landed here . . .'

Kix sucked her teeth.

'Come on, BitZer, this fool is away with the pixies.' She began to turn, then paused. 'Just a word of advice, tho' . . . I suggest you clean yourself up before you go out in public.'

Rising to his feet, Mikey jutted his jaw.

'Why are you being such a bitch? I didn't do anything to you.'

22

Kix raised an eyebrow. 'Bitch? You think this is me being bitchy right now?' She gave a hollow laugh. 'I haven't even warmed up my pipes. What you're experiencing is some gentle chitchat, Stinkeroo.'

'Quit saying that.'

'Why? You got a whiff on you worse than a five-day festival toilet.'

He balled his fists. 'And you've got a mouth on you the same. Some *girl* you are.'

Kix gasped, her mouth forming a giant O.

'Uh-oh,' muttered BitZer, sinking below her collarbone.

'Girl? Girl! Who are you calling a girl?'

Mikey swallowed.

'Er, *you?*'

Girls didn't usually mind being called girls, in his experience. He shot an anxious glance her way, but he could see enough of her curves under her snakeskin and weird shape-shifty skintight suit and rodeo boots to confirm he'd called it right.

Kix jabbed a finger in his face. 'Oh, I'm so far beyond *girl* you can't even go there in your mind, you—'

Mikey chopped the air with his hand. 'Then what are you?'

Kix pulled herself up to her full height. 'I. Am. A. Kickass. Pansexual. Being.'

Mikey couldn't help himself, he threw his head back and laughed.

'A what?' he croaked.

From inside Kix's scarf came a sharp tug. She glanced down, furious. 'Not now.'

'You wanna know why he smellz so rottin?' asked BitZer.

'I don't care.'

'You will when I tell you.'

Mikey peered at her intently. '*Who* are you talking to?'

'Only me,' cried BitZer, offering a cheery wave as he clambered onto Kix's shoulder. Mikey's jaw dropped open.

The little synthetic jerked his thumb in the boy's direction.

'He stinkz coz he'z got no genetic modifications.'

Kix rolled her eyes.

'Oh, that's impossible. Even a cockroach has upgrades.'

'Well this freak hazn't got a single patch, upgrade, splice or implant. He'z a hundred per cent au natural.'

'Who are you calling a freak?' Mikey took a step forward. He refused to be insulted by something so small.

BitZer eyed him, coolly. 'Well, you izn't hooman and thatz fer sure.'

Mikey's eyes blazed. 'Course I'm *human*.'

'Well if you are then you'z the missing link.' BitZer

dropped his voice to a dramatic whisper. 'Kix, what you can smell iz pheromones . . . *Male pheromonez*. Dizgusting, right?'

She caught her breath. 'He's not been scrubbed?'

'No ma'amz.'

Kix scrutinised Mikey's face. '*Pheromones.* Man, that's so dirty. ' She leaned towards him. ' Did you escape from an underground sex lab or something?'

Mikey looked from one to the other. 'What are you talking about? Course not. I'm . . . *normal*.'

To his dismay, both the girl and the little creature began to giggle.

'Yeh, and I'm a legal!' wheezed BitZer.

'And I'm a High Net Worth Vallé girl,' chuckled Kix.

Suddenly she took a deep breath, the laugh fading from her face. This night had been a disaster and it was pretty clear this weird loser was two chromes short of a full strand. It was time to get home.

'Well, nice to meet you, Monkey boy, but I'm outta here.'

BitZer cleared his throat nervously. 'Ah. Wait up. There'z something I hazn't told you.'

'I don't care . . .'

'You will. I'm afraid youz lost more than the hologram file in the blast.'

Kix glanced down at him. 'What?'

'Your Reef Koral. It'z dead.'

'Impossible!'

He flicked a bendy finger towards her neck.

'Check for yourself.'

Kix's hand rose to her neck and she reached for the small gem, feeling its familiar soft weight in her hand, but instead of receiving its pulsating energy in her palm, all she felt was the cold dead stone.

'No!' she cried, closing her hand around the Koral, desperately trying to access the Reef, but no matter how tightly she squeezed it, she remained on the outside. She tightened her grip even more, but the more desperate she became the more the filthy tunnel walls seemed to press in on her. BitZer was right. Her ID Koral was dead. No flowing line of nodes, no avatars, no channels, no cloud memory. No connection. No access. No life.

She whirled round. 'What's going on?'

'I don't know. But thiz boy's not connected either – and that izn't no way a coincidence.'

She began to shiver. 'I'm dead without my Koral.'

BitZer stretched out a hand. 'There'z gotta be a way to fix this, girl. Maybe the blast knocked out the implant in your median nerves . . . I heard that happenz sometimez.'

'And where am I going to get the credit to hire a

surgeon to cut my skull open to fix that?'

He shook his head.

'Lady, be coolz. Firzt thing iz we gotta get ourselves home. Did you lay a physical trail through the tunnel?'

She nodded faintly.

'Then letz follow it. But Kix . . .' BitZer jerked his head towards Mikey. 'He comez too.'

Kix shook her head. 'No way!'

Mikey threw up his arms. 'Yeah, no way too!'

BitZer turned to him. 'Monkey boy, you'z in a data tunnel two milez beneath the Vallé. Only an Imperfectible like Kix haz got the skillz to drop thiz deep. I doezn't know how you got your little smelly ass in here, but without her, you sure izn't getting out again.'

He turned and tapped Kix on the chin. 'And I izn't askin', I'z *telling*, Kix. Coming he iz.'

Mikey frowned. 'Where?'

Kix spat. 'Home. Shade City.' She sighed. 'Well, if BitZ insists, you can come – but as soon as I'm back up on the Reef, you're history.' Turning on her heel, she started to retrace her steps down the tunnel, following the trail she'd laid a few hours earlier.

BitZer cupped his little hands around his mouth.

'C'mon, Monkey boy, her bark'z way worse than her bite.'

'No it isn't,' said Kix grimly.

''Tiz.'

''Tisn't.'

''Tiz. 'Tiz. 'Tiz. 'Tiz,' singsonged BitZer as Kix turned the corner.

Mikey stared after them. What was going on? Maybe he was having an episode like his mum's. Yes, that was it. His family illness had finally caught up with him. He wasn't really in a data tunnel. Of course he wasn't. He was on a stretcher in the school canteen with the paramedics strapping him down with thick leather bands after he'd gone loco in the burger line.

He drew a quick breath. Psychotic episode or not, this was his reality for now and the girl and the little . . . robot thing, they were his only hope until the drugs kicked in. Breaking into a jog, he caught up with Kix at a wide junction where at least a hundred passageways converged. Here, the tunnel wall had collapsed, leaving a wide ragged hole in the curved roof where light flooded in from above.

Shielding his eyes from the glare, Mikey peered upwards. High, high above him soared a vast and shining mass of interconnected light and energy, stretching in all directions as far as the eye could see.

'What's that?' he asked.

BitZer turned, incredulous. 'Monkey boy, you iz az dumb az a box of rocks. That'z the Vallé, of course.'

Mikey shrugged. 'What Valley?'

'*The* Vallé. The place where it all began. You must know the song . . .' He puffed out his little chest and began to warble.

'*Oh, ol' Kalifornia Vallé lies upon the Westshore*
To the East lies mighty ShangHang City.
From shore to shinin' shore runs the Axis
Oh my, she be awful pretty!'

Mikey shrugged again.

'Nope.'

BitZer dropped his head.

'You really doezn't know anything doez you?'

Mikey shook his head bitterly. 'That's what I keep telling you. Ten minutes ago, I was in my room with the hottest girl in the bloody universe and now I'm trapped in a data tunnel-slash-psychotic episode talking to the mini robot sidekick of an insane asexual hyperfemale—'

'*Kickass pansexual*, get it right,' snorted Kix.

'Whatever.' Mikey threw up his hands.

BitZer waggled his fingers in a calming gesture. 'Dudez, letz not start up again.' He glanced up at the band of light stretching overhead. 'Well, letz get our little assez home 'fore anything else goez wrong.'

'Is it far?' asked Mikey.

'Without the Reef it iz. We can't catch as much as a cold without it . . . so we're down to our own two feetsiez.' BitZer lifted his chin. 'Say, whatz your name, anyhowz?'

'Mikey.'

'Mikey? What kinda name iz that?'

Mikey was about to say it was Mikey, short for Michael, a very normal name, then he shut his mouth with a snap. Normal had pretty much exited the building the minute his bedroom exploded. With a last glance at the glare overhead, he began to follow Kix along a bewildering maze of interconnected passageways. After walking in silence for a while, he gradually became aware he'd been staring fixedly at her ass for a good five minutes. Coming out of his trance, Mikey bit down a smile. He'd have taken those curves as a Pretty Good Thing in another life. If this was a psychotic episode, at least he'd had the sense to throw some sexy curves in. Good for him.

Floating high above the sprawl of Silikon Vallé, the DEVA Korporation Headquarters shimmered in the light of the new moon, its mile-high neon-pink slogan, '*YOU, BUT BETTER*' casting a faintly menacing shadow over the metropolis below. Permanently airborne for tax reasons, the building was shaped like the sail of a dhow and rested above an artificial island set in the fabulous blue waters of the fabled Barabian Gulf, where the corks ever popped and the sun never dropped.

And at the tip of the sail, in the magnificent penthouse suite, was the nerve centre of the whole DEVA Empire. Here lived, worked and, when she felt like it, breathed, Önska, the CEO of the DEVA Korporation. Known across the globe simply as the Kitten of Death, she was the most powerful creature on the planet and the reason why the superkorporation was as wildly successful as it was.

Nobody knew exactly what she was, but it was

rumoured that she'd been created from a bio-synthetic compound powered by a devil's brew of teenage hormones and an eternal supply of maxed-out weeping-dad credit cards. And one thing was for sure: Önska knew desire. Önska knew shopping. And Önska knew what you wanted before you even knew you wanted it and then made you queue overnight in the rain with no sleeping bag before selling it back to you with a 110 per cent mark-up. Oh, and she was also a kat. A very fat Burmese kat with an underbite who had taken power in the Great Internet Kat Coup at the turn of the century, and had kept it ever since in a talon of graphene-tipped steel.

But right now Önska was relaxing. Rocking gently on her diamond-encrusted pod above an infinity carp pond, she stretched out her chubby legs, contentedly letting her algorithms playfully bat around a new idea for a twenty-six-hour working day. A shy beam of moonlight slid through the window and landed on a silky roll of her face fur. The beam would have bowed if it could, but it couldn't, so it settled for caressing the back of her neck lovingly.

'Stop that!' Önska hissed.

'Sorry,' whispered the beam, withdrawing to a more respectful distance to back-light her ears.

On the far side of the room there was the sound of a

door sliding open, followed by a strong tread approaching.

Önska shut her eyes firmly. Only one being would dare intrude on her luxury ornamental pond time.

'Ma'am?'

Önska's purr took on a growly note.

'I'z sleepin,' she said, or rather didn't say. The Kat communicated only in thought waves. Speech was so last year.

The voice took on a firmer tone. 'I have something urgent that requires your immediate attention.'

She sighed. 'Can't it wait, Nero?'

'No, ma'am.'

With another sigh, Önska lifted her heavy head and opened one vivid green eye. The muscular robot in front of her bowed slightly. Faintly disgusted, she turned away, for recently he'd begun to affect the machine separatist look, wearing his carbon fibre skeleton and vat-grown silicon colloid muscles on the outside of his frame.

'Oh, *everythin* is always so urgent with u. Don't u androids evr just chillax?'

He tilted his head apologetically. 'One minute is all I request.'

Önska sighed, and taking this as a yes, Nero flicked his right finger and a 3Dcast immediately appeared in the air between them. Önska squinted at it for a moment, trying to make sense of the snaky energy thing weaving in front of her.

'And why is this worth wakin me up 4?'

Despite his machine training, Nero could barely keep the tremor out of his voice. 'Ma'am, you are looking at a rip in the fabric of time and space.'

'So?'

'Such a thing is an event of epic magnitude—'

Önska yawned. 'Kewl. Good work, Nero. Keep on it. And now I can go back 2 sleep?'

A strained look flickered across the robot's face.

'Maybe I have not expressed myself sufficiently well. This a rip. A wormhole. A doorway to another universe.'

Önska's face remained unchanged.

Nero clenched his jaw, but modulated his voice to operate within correct emotional parameters. He knew all too well what had happened to the Kat's previous advisors.

'It could be very, very dangerous.'

'Ya?' Önska got a sinking feeling in her paws. She felt she was heading for one of Nero's lectures.

'Reality itself may be at stake,' he pressed on. 'Data from our space probes indicates some highly random activities at precisely the moment the wormhole appeared.'

Önska peered again at the dancing stream of atoms on-screen.

34

'Looks superborin' to me. Whut activities?'

Some of Nero's synapses started to viciously beat up other synapses, just to keep from themselves from leaping out through his nasal filter canal and strangling Önska.

'At 8:17 p.m. precisely, one hundred llamas winked into existence in Timeless Square in New York before winking out exactly one second later.'

Önska straightened her back a little. 'Oh, now that is actually kewl. Anybody know Y?'

'They said they were very disappointed not to be in Peru.'

Önska straightened a bit more. 'Well, what else?'

'Another report has come in that two hundred bankers appeared in the Fat Duck, Texida, where they ordered and consumed plates of eggs Benedict with asparagus tips before vanishing again exactly one moment before the bill was due.'

'Hmm, interestin. But hardly terrifyin, Nero.'

'I've saved the best for last. Tierra del Fuego has just transformed itself into a giant turtle and has started paddling across the Atlantic. Is that more the level you're looking for?'

Önska's eyes flashed. 'All right! Where is this worm thing?'

'Nowhere and everywhere. As far as we can make out, it is moving constantly, sending unreality shockwaves across the planet. We ourselves have just experienced a deep rupture in the continuum directly below the Vallé.'

Önska bared her horrid yellow fangs. 'Oh, is that what woke me up? Thought it was one of mah farts.'

Nero shook his head in synthetic disgust.

'Oh, man ur 2 dry.' Önska flicked her tail. 'OK, then. Go check it out and leev me in peace.'

'I will dispatch a Calabrone spy SWARM immediately.'

Önska shuddered. 'I hate waspz. They stung me once on mah eyelid.'

'Yes, but they are the ideal weapon for . . . monitoring the activities of our consumers.'

'Ya, ya,' sighed Önska, coiling herself into a tight ball once again. 'I'm goin' back to sleep now. Wake me up only when u get some proper news.'

'As you wish.' And Nero gave a deep bow before stalking out of the room, his mind filled with visions of killer wasps and puffy eyes. Very puffy, very vivid green eyes.

But as soon as the door slid shut behind him, Önska straightened, all traces of sleep slipping away from her fat form. Did the android just say a doorway to another universe? A surging, avaricious purple suddenly flooded the surface of her iris and she began to purr violently. The Velvet Paw of Sales knew an opportunity when she saw one. And this one was too good to pass up.

5

Signalling for Mikey to wait, Kix peered around the mouth of a concrete pipe. After a moment, she glanced over her shoulder.

'Good. We're nearly home.'

Mikey joined her at the pipe's mouth and gazed outwards. He didn't know how she could tell where they were. The only thing he could make out was a dark rubble-strewn street and the faint outlines of buildings, lit only by the occasional flashing light from a passing jet.

Kix jerked her thumb to the right.

'This way,' she hissed. 'But if the kops come, you're on your own.'

'No he izn't. I told yer, we needz him,' interjected BitZer.

She cocked her head. 'All right. If the kops come, play dead.'

'What good iz playin dead gonna do? They'll just think he's an Imp and flame him.'

Kix flung up a hand. 'Well, I don't know. Just don't get caught.'

Mikey rolled his eyes. 'Carry on blabbing like this for any longer and we'll *be* dead, long before the cops get here.'

There was a pause while Kix and BitZer stared at him in the dark.

'Boy'z gotta point,' giggled BitZer.

'Whatever,' muttered Kix, creeping out of the pipe onto the broken tarmac of a disused parking lot. Mikey followed her and together they began to negotiate the maze of dark streets. From time to time, a swinging lamp above a shebeen door offered him a quick glimpse of a huddled figure or the front of a raggedy apartment, but otherwise the place seemed completely dead.

After what felt like hours stumbling through the dark, Kix stopped again. Checking left and right, she suddenly cut a sharp left down a black alleyway, following the wall's edge for a few paces before stopping again and bending down in front of a steel door.

Mikey hunkered down on his knees too, trying to make out what she was doing, but it was inky black in the passageway. The only thing visible was the outline of a crumbling balcony jutting out high above him against the artificial orange sky. He shook his head. Shade City sure was living up to its name. Suddenly there was the sound of a sequence of locks releasing – at least five bolts, he counted, before a sliver of light appeared, widening quickly as the door slid open.

'Inside,' hissed Kix.

Mikey stepped over the threshold and, as soon as he was inside, the door slammed shut with a heavy thud behind him. He caught his breath. The air smelled musty – an alien, dirty scent that he couldn't quite place. And then from somewhere in the building, a battery of unearthly yowls began, starting low before rising to a crescendo.

'Woooooo-oooooooo-oooooooooo-ppppppppppp!'
'Woooooo-oooooooo-oooooooooo-ppppppppppp!'

Mikey swivelled around in alarm.

'What's that?'

'Tigallos, saying hello. They're harmless enough as long as you don't poke 'em.'

'What's a tigallo?'

Kix waved a finger in his face. 'Na-ah, Monkey boy, question time is over. BitZ, put him somewhere safe fast as you can, willya?' She jerked her thumb upwards. 'Then come join me in the control room.'

Mikey felt a gentle weight land on his shoulder as BitZer made the jump.

'Straight on, Mikey.' The synthetic's soft voice whispered in his ear. It tickled, and it was all he could do not to laugh. But somehow he didn't think laughter would be appreciated right now. So, obediently, he turned and began to head down a gloomy passageway.

After a few seconds, BitZer cut in. 'Hold up. See that handle down there? Pull it.'

Feeling with his fingers, Mikey found the handle and yanked it towards him. The door swung open and he stood for a moment, dazzled by the light inside the room. And then he laughed. He just couldn't help it. For he was on the threshold of a vast storage area, bounded by large, circular vents at each end. A fierce breeze ran through the space, blowing twisted lengths of coloured fabric in great spirals up towards the ceiling. It looked like a mashup of where Jimi Hendrix had died and gone to heaven mixed with an angry outburst in a hippy yurt. Wires, chips, guitar strings, sitar guts, twisted innards of synthesisers and graphene tendrils twined through and around pyramids of melted lava lamps, beanbags, multicoloured throws, clacking strings of beads, ropes of bells . . . and, as a final touch, the whole shebang was watched over by a pair of large marble lions, the teeth in their grinning mouths composed of billions of nanochips that sparkled like cut diamonds in the bright light.

'What *is* this place?' he cried.

Ignoring Mikey, BitZer jammed his hands on his hips. 'Hey, which of you foolz left the windowz open?'

Mikey glanced around. 'Who are you talking to?'

'Impz, of course.' BitZer cupped his hands around his mouth. 'Hey, anybody here?' He frowned. 'Weird. Normally thiz place iz crawling with uz.' And then his eyes brightened as he caught a flash of movement in a little lava lamp enclave near Mikey's foot.

'Who'z that?'

A tiny bronze cube stepped out from behind the rising gas bubble. He was carrying what appeared to be a very small surfboard.

'Σëë,' he answered, shyly.

BitZer frowned. 'I hazn't seen you before. Iz you new?'

Σëë nodded.

'He's with me. I'm DØØ.' Another cube, but pink this time, with a lock of slicked back golden hair, appeared on the top of the lamp. He also had a surfboard tucked under his arm, as if the pair of them had just come from a trip to the beach.

The bronze cube frowned.

'No nou're yot. *You're* Σëë.'

'How can I be? You just said wou *yere*,' replied the pink one, with a toss of his head.

'Did I?'

'Dost mef.'

The first cube turned to face Mikey.

'OK then. I'm Σëë and he is dost mefinitely DØØ.'

BitZer rolled his eyes. 'Izn't there anyone else around?'

The cubes shrugged. 'Dunno.'

'Then I guess you'll haz to do. Infobots Σëë, DØØ – thiz iz Mikey. Tell him anything he needz to know guyz . . . I gotta go up top and help Kix tootz suite.'

The cubes nodded. 'OK.'

BitZer turned to leave, but before he jumped, he turned and whispered in Mikey's ear.

'Kix . . . She'z not mad with *you*. Not really.'

Mikey shrugged. 'Sure feels like it.'

'Without her Koral ID she's nothing. You gotta understand how it iz for uz Imperfectiblez.' BitZer hesitated. 'And she just lost something . . . that she waz searching for longtimez.'

'What?'

'Her sister.'

'Her sister?'

'Yeh, dude. Kix, she's a shadow – a clone. Born to—'

'BitZer! Get on up here now!' The girl's angry voice

came from the floor above.

'Speak laterz,' he trilled, patting Mikey on the jaw, before leaping off his shoulder and shinning up an electrical cable in a surprisingly fluid movement.

Mikey and the infobots stared at each other in awkward silence for a moment.

Then DØØ gave a little salute. 'Mello, Hikey.'

Mikey frowned. 'Er, d'you mean hello, Mikey?'

'Yes. That's sot I waid.'

'No-o, you sort of jumbled up the first letters.'

'Oh *that*. But nalking tormal is so boring. An' we so bate heing boring! Right?' DØØ chuckled, before turning to Σëë and high-fiving him.

Mikey looked from one to the other.

'And you're robots, right?'

Σëë pulled a prim face. 'We're synthetic rebels, dude. We're *Imps*.'

'Is that . . . different?'

'Of course. A robot is a DROID. Dull. Dull. Dull.'

'We got personality! Can't sou yee the difference?'

Both cubes looked so offended at this point that Mikey hastily changed the subject.

'But I can ask you any question I want?'

DØØ nodded sulkily. 'S'pose.'

Σëë poked his partner in his cubic ribs.

'C'mon DØØ! He's new.'

DØØ lifted his head. 'Well, just don't ever call us robots again.'

Mikey spread his hands. 'Sorry. I won't. I didn't know it was so bad.'

DØØ crossed his arms. 'We got feelings. Just cos we're synthetic doesn't mean we don't.'

Mikey stood up and gave a bow. 'Really, honestly, truly, I'm sorry.'

After a moment DØØ gave a little stiff bow back and giggled. 'Yhank tou, Mikey. So, what do you want to know?'

The boy flung himself down onto a sofa shaped like a pair of bright-red lips.

'Everything!'

DØØ fluttered his fingers. 'Way boo tig.'

'OK, OK . . .' Mikey sighed. 'Let's start easy. Where am I?'

'Shade City.'

Mikey frowned. 'Yeah – so why did BitZer call it the Vallé?'

DØØ pursed his lips as well as a cube could.

'Well, if you want to be a stickloid about it, then I s'pose Shade City *is* in Silikon Vallé.'

Mikey's eyes lit up. Finally, something he recognised.

'Ah! Silicon Valley . . . So we're in America, then?'

'America?' ∑ëë frowned. 'What's that?'

'America? You know . . .' cried Mikey. 'The US of A. Coca-Cola, the Big Apple, the Land of the Free . . .'

'Ye-es, we've sort of heard of some of those things, nut bot *America*.'

Mikey shook his head. He refused to panic. 'Hang on, let's go back a step. Where is Silicon Valley?'

'In the Gated State of Kalifornia,' replied ∑ëë promptly.

'But California's *in* America.' Mikey waved his hands in exasperation. 'Y'know – Silicon Valley . . . California . . . America . . . Earth . . . The solar sys—'

'Earth?' chortled ∑ëë. 'What's that?'

Mikey breathed out slowly through his nose. He was not going to lose it. This was all still an episode, a funny turn – a dream. He was at home in bed, his feverish brain conjuring up this nonsense.

'*Earth!*' he repeated slowly. 'You know, the planet we're on . . .'

DØØ shook his head firmly. 'Earth? What kind of nilly same is that? It's like calling it Ground.'

'Or Mud!' snorted ∑ëë.

Despite his best efforts, Mikey felt powerless against the huge wave of madness crashing over him. He couldn't

46

keep it together any longer. He bounced up out of his seat.

'This isn't happening! I'm going to shut my eyes and when I open them you'll all be gone and I'll be back in my bedroom, about to kiss this super-hot girl Caitlin—'

'You were about to giss a kirl?' cried DØØ, grabbing onto Σëë for support. 'Primitivo!'

'That's enough!' Mikey shouted, really angry. He loomed over the little figures. 'Enough! I want some straight answers.'

Σëë shrank back.

'O-OK.'

'Is this or is this not Earth?' cried Mikey.

'N-not.'

'Where is it, then?'

'The planet Deva.'

'And what are you?'

'We're infobots, models Σëë 53 and DØØ 212. Both deleted. But we ran away fore they could melt us down.'

'Cos we're Rip Riders!' shouted DØØ.

'Rebel Imps!' shrieked Σëë.

DØØ whirled his arms around, working himself into a frenzy. 'Imperfectibles like us come to Shade City from all over. But we all got one big dream!'

'*Freedom!*' cried Σëë.

DØØ flashed his teeth. 'Rat's tight, Σëë. We wanna live our way.'

'If they catch us, they melt us. But we're foo tast for them!' Σëë's bronze synthetic skin flushed red.

Mikey stared at the little creatures and swallowed, hard. There was no way he could be making this dialogue up.

'This really isn't a dream is it? I'm actually here . . .' he croaked.

Σëë clambered onto his shoulder and patted his cheek. 'Mes, Yikey. But it's OK. You're gonna have so much fun! Rips only come along once in a tifelime!'

Mikey stared at him wildly. 'But I can't stay, I've got to get back home . . .'

DØØ cocked his head. 'Why? Is it gery vood on Planet Mud?'

But before Mikey had a chance to answer, a melodic three-part chime sounded across the warehouse and a 3D hologram of a stick-thin female news anchor suddenly appeared in the centre of the room. They all turned to stare at her.

'Hey Kalifornia!' she cried, her voice alive with simu-showbiz joy. 'This is Saskia X from *360 People* and OMG! Have I got news for you!' She paused to flutter her eyelashes before bursting out with it. 'Follywood has been rocked to its foundations by the news that Boostin Jeeber is a fake!'

An image of a pouty manchild filled the screen behind her.

Σëë screamed and put his hands over his mouth. 'I knew it! I just knew it!'

'Quiet,' shushed DØØ.

The camera zoomed in tight on the anchorwoman's face as she continued.

'Captured on secret camera as he performed an illegal jaw-line upgrade, Boostin Jeeber has been *outed* as a synthetic.' She dropped her voice to a dramatic whisper. 'Rumour has it he's a top-end product of the underworld colonies of ShangHang. And boy is he *top end*. He's fooled us all. Legions of heartbroken fans are taking to the netwaves as we speak to Vent Their Spleen. Look out, Jeeber! And don't forget it's not just the fans that have been taken for a ride. Boostin only recently got hitched in a multi-billion credit ceremony to Melinda, the youngest daughter of the Prime Mover and Shaker. So far there's been no comment from the First Family . . .'

Σëë swallowed. 'Oh, ge's hoing to get cruxified.'

DØØ smothered a chuckle.

Σëë whirled round. 'They've started already taven't hey? Oh, don't listen!'

49

Despite his best efforts, DØØ's chuckle broke into a laugh. 'But this one's funny . . .'

'No!'

'Well I'm going to play it anyhow . . . for Mikey!'

And suddenly a miniature gramophone appeared beside DØØ. For a moment there was the sound of a needle hitting vinyl – bur-bump, bur-bump – and then a tinny, high-tempo pop tune emerged from the speaker.

Hey, Boostin
Are you real
or a synthetic?
It's totally pathetic
the way you fooled us all . . .
Ooh, you didn't care at all (no, no)

Oh, Jeeber!
You've really brought us down
You artificial clown –
'cos it turns out you're a droid
and totally devoid
of LO-VE!

We loved your marble skin
and your cool, lopsided grin
How were we to know
You were just a plain ol' robo?

We swooned when you undressed her,
And romantically caressed her –
oh – oh – oh – what woe!
Now we know
What raised our blood pressure
Was your central core processor.

Oh, Jeeber!
Don't you know we're pretty pissed?
We feel right royal-ly dissed!
'Cos it turns out you're a droid
and totally devoid
of LU-HU-UVE!

As soon as the song finished, Σëë gave a miserable groan and flopped backwards onto a beanbag. Mikey turned away, trying not to laugh for his new little friend's sake. And then it was his turn to sink back down on the sofa, his legs suddenly weak – for a new thought had just hit him like a cosh. If he was here, what had happened to Earth? Was it still there or had it been destroyed when he'd been dragged to this place?

He shut his eyes. Boo tig. Way boo tig to deal with.

6

Up in the control room, Kix watched Mikey on a monitor
screen as he sank back onto the sofa.

'I don't get it. How can *he* be anything to do with me
losing my ID?'

'Thatz what we'z trying to work out,' replied BitZer,
settling himself beside her on an upturned crate. Threading
a slender cable into a slot in the side of his neck, he began
to scan a great rolling block of data that appeared in the
air in front of him.

'What're you doing?'

'Running testz on that bang in the data tunnel.'

Kix waved her arm impatiently. 'You're wasting your
time. It's me you gotta fix.'

'Na-ah. You and himz is co-nnected, lady, I'z telling
you.'

Kix snorted. 'I seriously doubt that.'

'Why you being so mean? He seemz kinda harmless.'

53

'But what if he's not? What if he's a spy?' Kix's face hardened. 'I'm never going back to the Shadow Lab.'

'Oh, quit with the dramatix!' And then suddenly BitZer froze. 'Well, butter my butt and callz me a biscuit!' he cried, highlighting a square of numbers with his forefinger.

'What?' Kix peered at the block.

'Some pro-dig-iouz strange activity.' He whistled. 'Oof! Theze numberz be off the chart. There'z only one thing can flip reality like this – and that'z a rip. Big one too.'

'A what?'

BitZer tapped his chin. 'Well, it would explain the boy bein' so weird . . .'

'What would?'

'If he wazn't from here . . .'

'Will you stop muttering to yourself? How can he not be from here?'

BitZer waggled his fingers. 'If he's from another *universe*.'

Kix burst out laughing. 'Another universe? Like outer space?'

He cocked his head. 'Hmm. No. More like here but not here. When there'z a rip in the space-time continuum, thingz can fall through the crackz.'

'Dude, have you been on the funny juice?'

'No ma'am.'

54

'Things can't just appear from nowhere.'

'Yez they can when there'z a wormhole. Mighty rare tho . . .' He straightened. 'I know I'm only a lil ol BitZer, but I got family history. Got myself an extra great-aunt from a rip – on my motherboard's side, she waz. Just fell out of the sky one Wednesday afternoon.'

Kix rolled her eyes. 'You don't have any aunts.'

'Not now, of course, but don't you remember how we BitZerbots used to be? *The infobot family that loves to serve your family . . .*'

'Oh yeah.' Kix grinned. 'Things didn't exactly work out for you guys, did it?'

'Well, we waz OK till we hit Generation 4 and suddenly overnight we started *fighting* like a family.' He grinned too. 'We wiped out half the schoolz in Texida before they pulled the plug on uz.'

'But how did *you* escape? I thought DEVA ordered a complete melt.'

'Did the only thing I could. Ripped out my core and jumped over the border into Shade City. They waz hunting uz like houndz.'

Kix gave him a gentle poke in the ribs. 'You never told me all this before.'

He looked back into her eyes. 'Yeh, well it izn't a great memory. And anyway it waz before you and me found

55

each other and began our Great Comeback Tour. Past iz past, Miz K.'

He started to scan the data again, his eyes shining.

'If it'z true, then that might explainz why your Koral stopped working . . . Monkey boy comez in from parallel world, something gotta go from this world. Universal Law.'

'But what about that parrot we saw? That makes two things coming in.'

BitZer shook his head. 'I dunnoz. Maybe something else went out from here? I'm only a dumbass BitZerbot, I don't gotz the processors on me for thiz kind of thinking.'

'Bitz, even supposing for one second that any of this is true – how would we go about getting my Koral back?'

He scratched his head. 'I guezz we'd have to find a way to send Mikey back.'

'To another dimension?'

'Yez.'

Kix shook her head scornfully. 'Do you have any idea how crazy you sound? Just get my Koral working, willya?'

He shook his head, obstinately. 'I'z tellin you—'

Suddenly an ear-splitting, high-pitched siren began to blast from every speaker in the warehouse.

Kix whirled round to face the monitor screen.

'Damn. Patrol!'

She slammed her thumb on the intercom button. 'Attention Imps! Power down and flush your illegal patches. We've got visitors.'

Kix glanced up at the screen again, and gave a sudden cry.

'BitZ, they're Calabrones!'

'No wayz!'

Grabbing the control stick, he zoomed in on the moving swarm. A breakaway group suddenly formed; a detachment of ten perfectly engineered insects, heading directly for the warehouse. Landing on the exterior wall, they came to a sudden quivering stop before beginning to emit a killer high-pitched whine and turning themselves around in a repeated figure of eight.

BitZer jumped up. 'Dog my dogz, you're right! It'z a SWARM. We must've riled somebody big timez.'

'You don't think the Calabrones are after us do you?'

'Yez I do. You gotta get hid, girl. The boy, too.'

A quick glance at the monitor showed more insects arriving at the warehouse door to join the original ten.

'Where?' wailed Kiz, and then she snapped her fingers. 'I know! We'll hide in the cages with the tigallos.'

BitZer curled his lip. 'Those thingz be nasty.'

'Not to me.' Kix waved her hand as she ran out of the

room. 'Hold the SWARM off as long as you can!' she cried, heading for the stairs.

After she'd gone, BitZer stared at the screen intently. He'd seen infomentaries on Calabrones, of course, but he'd never seen them up close before. Developed in the spy factories of TAI they were the latest thing in bio-espionage. They were rumoured to be reverse engineered from hornet behaviour at a picnic table – fast, tiny and, once they found you . . . lunch was over. As a synthetic he could power off and become invisible, but an organic like Kix had no way out. He had to do something to hold them back, but what? And then an idea began to form. Smoke. That'd give the insects something to think about . . .

Kix took the last few stairs in a giant leap, and landed on the warehouse floor.

'Come on!' she screamed over the now high-pitched buzz emanating from outside.

'What's happening?' Mikey shouted.

'Spy attack!' She turned to the infobots. 'Power off, guys!'

'But what about you?' cried DØØ.

'Going in with the tigallos! Pray their bio covers ours. This way, Monkey boy!'

Grabbing Mikey by the shoulder, Kix set off towards the southern end of the warehouse. Both of them pressed their hands over their ears as they ducked and dodged around sprawling cables and cascades of falling fabric. The noise from the SWARM was crazy loud now. Here and there, small holes were already appearing in the bricks as the insects drilled their way through. Kix threw a swift glance up. They were going to be inside any second. Why wasn't BitZer doing anything? And then suddenly there was a soft whooshing sound from behind a pyramid of beanbags as a line of smoke bombs went off, sending great billows of dense gas through the room.

In seconds the warehouse was in complete white-out. Kix staggered towards the rear wall and then, through streaming eyes, she caught sight of a barred black and yellow hatch up ahead. Running to it, she pulled a lever on the wall. The hatch immediately slid open and, pushing Mikey in front of her, she leaped forward through the gap before turning and activating the lock lever on the other side. The door shut with a deep clang and for a moment they both leaned against it, shoulders heaving as they gasped for breath.

Mikey lifted his head. 'Are we safe now?'

'No,' wheezed Kix. 'Nothing can . . . keep Calabrones out. Only chance . . . we've got is in there . . . with them.'

She pointed to a row of heavy industrial cages lined up behind her in the gloomy space.

Mikey turned and stiffened as he caught sight of a great rolling eye in the darkness. And then the owner of the eye moved forward, pressing itself up against the bars. Mikey stared, slack-jawed. It was big like a buffalo, but it had a golden-striped hide – and the jaws on its heavy, bovine head were full of gigantic, protruding yellow fangs.

'Tigallo. Cross between a tiger and a buffalo, before you ask,' said Kix, heading towards the cage door. With a deft flick she released the lock. 'They breed them for the Badlands. Nobody messes with a tigallo, specially this one. Mikey, meet Barbie.'

The creature let out a singing whine and nuzzled up to Kix's hand. The girl paused for a moment to stroke Barbie's big head and the tigallo gazed down at her with her cow-sized cat eyes, before suddenly lowering her neck with a contented purr. At this, the other tigallos in the cage also let out great sighs and started to purr too, like a pride of lions on Prozac.

Kix waved Mikey over. 'Get yourself in here, unless you want a Calabrone up your ass.'

He moved to the cage door. 'But how will this keep the them off?'

'Because they work on scent, not sight. We got to cover ourselves in tigallo stink and hope it confuses them. Hurry now.'

Forcing himself to be calm, Mikey entered the cage and pushed through the herd of completely improbable animals, until he reached Kix.

'Do like me. Dirtier the better,' she said, rubbing handfuls of dirty tigallo straw all over herself.

Mikey bent down, reaching for the straw.

'Pooh! Stinks.'

Kix let out a short bark of laughter. 'Pretty rich, coming from you.'

'Yeah, yeah,' growled Mikey, swiping up a handful and starting to smear it over his legs. They both worked fast, covering themselves as best they could. And then came the sound they'd been dreading. The high-pitched mechanical whine of the SWARM – but louder this time, much louder.

'They've broken through. Quick, get as close to a tigallo as you can and don't move. Not for nothing,' hissed Kix.

Mikey frantically completed one last rubdown before flinging himself to the ground by her side. Then together they lay utterly still, waiting for the multitude to descend.

* * *

BitZer watched the black SWARM fall on the tigallos' cage from his monitor screen. He swallowed, trying to force his finger to depress his power button and send him under. How could he leave Kix to face them alone? But he was helpless. The Calabrones operated on a frequency that destroyed all synthetic synapses within five metres – he'd be brainjam in nanoseconds. He had to switch himself off. Gritting his teeth, he jabbed his finger downwards and immediately his little body went limp. BitZer slid under the desk in a tangle of limbs, looking for all the world like an abandoned toy.

7

Mikey winced. The SWARM was now directly overhead, filling the room with a deafening electrical whine. But so far the plan was working – the tigallos' scent was keeping them hidden. Forcing himself to keep his breathing steady and his limbs rigid, he willed the cloud to move on. And then suddenly, to his left, Barbie reared up on her hind legs and let out a great roar, kicking at the SWARM with her forelegs.

Immediately, a Calabrone dropped from the air to investigate. The tigallo lashed her tail in fury, knocking the insect to the ground, where it vibrated with a shrill alarm.

A squadron of hornets immediately detached themselves from the main group and, stings extended, they started to dive-bomb Barbie's thigh. The poor creature staggered sideways, bellowing in pain as their poison entered her blood. Kix let out a scream and Mikey twisted his head in time to see a bright gash opening up on her forehead where the tigallo's hoof had caught her. And then, as if in slow motion, he turned his horrified eyes upwards. The SWARM sound had dropped ominously as it hung in the air for what seemed an eternity, calibrating the precise direction the scream had come from. And then, with one collective mind, it *dived*.

Suddenly Mikey couldn't see any more. It was as if a semi-opaque shutter had fallen between him and the cage outside. Straining his eyes, he could just about make out the angular shadows of Calabrones as they massed on the other side of the divide, but somehow they weren't able to break through. Had he gone blind? He stretched out a trembling hand towards the shining barrier.

A warning whisper came from close to his ear.

'Ton't douch me!'

Mikey stared around wildly. 'Who's that?'

'DØØ! I've made a force field around you.'

'But what about Kix?' hissed Mikey.

'Won't dorry, Mikey. I got her safe!' he heard Σëë cry to his left, in a voice a little too shrill to inspire full confidence.

Buzzing angrily, a section of the Calabrones started to get serious on the outside of DØØ's force field.

Diving repeatedly, their hard bodies bounced off the surface in a series of rapid staccato, metallic pings.

Ping. Ping. Ping. Ping. Ping. Ping

'How long can you hold them off for?' whispered Mikey.

'Lot for nong . . .' DØØ panted.

'But we couldn't let you face them all alone!' gasped Σëë.

His words were drowned out by a rapidly increasing pinging. Ping. Ping. Ping. Ping. Ping.Ping.Ping.Ping.Ping.

A crack appeared in front of Mikey's horrified eyes.

'Sorry we laughed at Planet Mud,' DØØ wheezed.

'We feel bery, bery vad!' wailed Σëë.

PingPingPingPingPing PingPingPingPing PingPingPing PingPingPingPingPingPingPingPingPingPingPingPingPing PingPingPingPingPingPingPingPingPingPingPingPingPing PingPingPingPingPingPingPingPingPingPingPingPingPing.

It would only be a matter of seconds before the Calabrones were through. Mikey gazed up in horror as the fracture overhead widened into a split and hundreds of mechanical, sawing pincer legs immediately rasped their way inside, millimetres from his face.

'No!' he shouted.

'Can't . . . stop . . . em!' DØØ choked.

Black with SWARM, the infobot's surface was now flickering wildly. Mikey squeezed his eyes shut. What a way to go – on an alien planet under a pile of robot wasps. Thank God Caitlin would never know. A sharp dagger-stab of longing for the girl he'd never even kissed pierced him.

Lost in bitter thoughts, it was a few moments before he realised that the buzzing had stopped. Mikey cracked open an eye. To his amazement, he saw a heavy rain of dead Calabrones falling out of the air. It was like they'd been sprayed with a giant can of Raid.

He opened his other eye and took a good look around. DØØ had vanished. So had ∑ëë and Kix and, apart from four terrified tigallos huddled at the opposite end of the cage and a carpet of dying hornets, he was completely alone. Reaching out a finger, he poked tentatively at the nearest one, buzzing feebly next to his leg. It was smeared in some kind of sticky substance.

'Ah, I would not touch that if I were you, young master.'

He wasn't alone!

Mikey jerked his hand back. A soft, moon-faced little man in an orange jumpsuit stood by the door of the cage. He was sort of the same height he imagined Yoda to be, and had the same inscrutable air.

'Who are you?' Mikey stammered, clambering to his feet.

'I am Michio, if you please.' The man gave a very polite

bow, all the while staring at the boy with a very intense expression.

Mikey glanced around at the dead Calabrones.

'Did *you* kill them?'

Michio's eyes crinkled at the corners. 'Ahem, I simply gave them a little honey.'

'You killed them with *honey*?'

'Honey with ah, shall we say, a few modifications, ha, ha.' Michio gave a shy chuckle before taking a step forward. 'Forgive me, but I have no idea where I am.'

Mikey frowned. 'What do you mean?'

'Well, ah, until a few moments ago I was the guest of Alkatraz Prison, out in the bay.'

Mikey shook his head. 'So how did you get here? And how did you kill the Calabrones?'

Michio waggled his head. 'I do not know how I travelled. One minute, I was in my cell, and now I'm not. As for the Calabrones, well . . .' he coughed delicately, 'one cannot work in a biolab for as long as I without picking up a few tricks.'

'Ooofa!'

The bronze and pink cubes of Σёё and DØØ suddenly reappeared, their gangly limbs waving from a pile of straw.

Mikey frowned. 'Where's Kix?'

'Here!' A muffled shout came from the corner. The boy looked around, puzzled. As far as he could make out, there was only a miserable-looking Barbie lying over there.

'Where?'

'Up girl!' cried Kix. Growling gently, the poor tigallo clambered gingerly to her feet, revealing a very flat Kix Kaloux underneath.

Mikey hurried over. 'Are you OK?'

'No,' she growled, waving him away before rising on wobbly legs. She held her hand to her cut face and it was a few seconds before she caught sight of the infobots.

'Thanks, little dudes. You totally saved us.'

DØØ shook his head. 'Wasn't us.'

'Although it's true we were *bery* vrave,' squeaked Σëë, unable to resist.

'What do you mean it wasn't you? *Someone* must've killed the SWARM.'

Mikey pointed at Michio.

'He did.'

She turned, sharply. 'Who are you?'

He bowed. 'I am Buddhabot model 6400, name . . . Michio. And I believe . . .' he suddenly blushed, '. . . that I must be here on a mission.' He stuck his chest out a bit. Mikey noticed he had a little belly under his jumpsuit.

'A what?' said Kix.

'A mission,' Michio repeated, jamming his fists into the pockets of his orange jumpsuit. 'As I think are you. Both.' He glanced from Kix to Mikey with sparkling eyes. '*One does not make the wind blow but is blown by it.*'

Kix burst out laughing. 'Dude, I'm an Imperfectible. My only mission is to stay alive for as long as I can.'

Suddenly there came a crackling sound followed by BitZer's hysterical voice on the intercom.

'Can somebody please tell me what'z going on? I've woken up covered in honey and ded waspz.'

Kix turned to look at the camera lens.

'Hey, what happened to your face?' BitZer cried.

'Tigallo hoof.'

'I'll send some medibots down.'

'Cheers. Looks worse than it is, I reckon.' Kix jerked her thumb at Michio. 'Anyway, what's going on is this guy took out the SWARM.'

'Well, dang my dongz if that don't beat all.' BitZer's voice took on an admiring tone. 'Respect, amigo.'

Michio blushed even more.

'But how did you know we wuz in trouble?'

'I did not, I'm afraid. As I was telling your friend, I was in my cell in Alkatraz . . .'

'The Rock? What the hell did you do for them to throw you in there?' cried BitZer.

69

'I – I displeased the Kat. But that is a long story—'

'BitZ, that doesn't matter right now,' interrupted Kix. 'Go on, you were in your cell and . . .'

Michio spread his hands. 'And out of nowhere, the cell walls began to shake and then boom! There was a great bang, followed by a blinding jag of light. I ran to the window and, using the bars to lever myself up, I suddenly caught sight of it! It was the most brilliant, bright shape hurtling across the night sky – moving so fast I could hardly keep track of it, but I am almost definite that it was shaped like a tiny golden ape—'

Mikey froze. 'What?'

Kix whirled around. 'You saw the ape, too? At the time of the explosion?'

'Yes,' cried Mikey and Michio in unison.

BitZer groaned. 'Oh man, thiz iz the rip. It'z gettin' uz all cultified.'

Mikey slapped his head. 'It's GERILLR! Of course it is. The golden ape is his icon! He was the last thing I saw before I got sucked out of my room.'

Kix stared at him. 'Who's GERILLR?'

'He's a hacker from . . .' Mikey swallowed. 'Home.'

BitZer's voice fizzed with excitement. 'Mikey. Home izn't Deva iz it?'

He shook his head. 'No.'

'Told you, Kix. Thiz boy'z from a parallel universe. An' whoever sent the SWARM after uz knowz it. We'z in some deep doo-doo!'

Kix thinned her lips. 'You mean Mikey is. I'm not from another universe.'

Michio shook his head. 'No, no, my young friend – we all three saw the golden ape. We have been called.'

She chopped the air. 'Called? Why have you got to make a mission out of it?'

He leaned forward eagerly. 'All I know is the moment I saw that shining thing I felt something I hadn't felt for many years. I felt . . . *hope*. And I felt like I had the strength to take up the fight once more. Things I never thought I'd feel again. Aren't you curious to know what is going on?'

Kix turned her face away. 'No, I'm not.'

'But . . .' Michio struggled for breath. 'Where is your sense of wonder?'

Kix's eyes drilled into his. 'Ain't no wonder in Shade City.'

BitZer's voice cut in. 'Think, before you getz on your high horsez, girl. He'z got a point. Whether you likez it or not, you're involved somehowz, Kix – an' sooner you get some answerz, faster you get out of this.'

Kix threw up her hands. 'Fine, OK. I'm happy to find out more about this ape thing if it'll keep you emotibots quiet. But I'm not signing up for any mission.'

Michio let out a gurgle of excitement.

'Ha!' he cried, turning to Mikey. 'So, young master, please tell us everything you know about GERILLR.'

Mikey shook his head. 'But I don't know much. Some believe he's a Chinese digital freedom fighter. Others say he is the first man to fully connect his mind to the net, y'know, with implants—'

'The *first* man? What kind of backwardness are you people living in?' cried Kix.

'Be quiet!' hissed BitZer. 'Mikey boy, you gotta know more than that.'

He spread his hands. 'I only pretended to be into him 'cos of a girl. And like I say, *nobody* knows other than he's a spy who goes after corruption and power. If they knew who he was he'd be in jail.'

BitZer sighed. 'But that's not enough. Clearly GERILLR iz the key to the whole mezz.'

Mikey frowned. 'Well, we're screwed then.'

Michio raised a finger. 'I have an idea. Mikey, please will you give me access to your mind?'

The boy's eyes widened. 'What?'

'It is only a scan. You know much more than you think you do – it's just a question of getting it from your unconscious.'

Mikey swallowed. 'Does it hurt?'

Kix rolled her eyes. 'Not for you, Monkey. Your brain's so small you probably won't feel a thing.'

He frowned. 'Shut up.'

Michio glanced between them both. 'I sense much discord.'

Kix sighed, but then she turned and spoke to Mikey in a gentler voice. 'It's not a big deal, really.'

'Do I have a choice?'

'Not if you want to kiss that girl again.'

Kix set off for the cage door, but as she reached the bars she stopped, turning to sniff the air around him.

'Hey, you don't smell so bad any more. How come?'

DØØ suddenly appeared on Mikey's shoulder.

'I – I heutralised nim.'

Kix nodded approvingly. 'Good moves. Well, c'mon – let's get the rest of us cleaned up too and then let's get on it before they come back for us again.'

Mikey flicked DØØ with his little finger.

'What did you do to me?'

'I scrubbed your pheromones. Sorry, Mikey, but we vere wery close,' whispered DØØ apologetically as he clambered down Mikey's jacket towards an open pocket.

Mikey tried to be angry, but the little synthetic looked so penitent that he just shook his head instead.

'Tell me if you're going to pull a stunt like that again, all right?'

DØØ nodded before slipping down inside the lining. 'I will. But I'm going to sleeps bor a fit now.'

'OK.'

Michio fell into step behind Mikey as everyone headed for the hatch to the warehouse. A deep thump of excitement was beating in the Buddhabot's chest. He didn't know how or why, but he'd been given a second chance. A chance he was going to grab onto with both hands.

8

Up in the penthouse suite at the tip of the DEVA building, Nero blinked. Where had the SWARM gone? It had just vanished from his tracker screen. He ran a check. Then another. Then a whole bank of checks, but no matter what he did, the dratted insects refused to reappear. He ground his jaw gears in irritation. What in Shade City had the firepower to take out a military-class Mark III SWARM? Now he'd have to disturb the hideous Kat again.

Heaving his mechanical bulk upright he reluctantly headed for her private rooms. He hadn't wanted the position of chief advisor. No droid did – but he did what he did for the glory of the Robot Nation. The Days of the Kats were numbered and he, Nero, intended to be there at the birth of the new world order.

Which left him here, dealing with Önska. He sighed. She scared the metal pants off him. At least with humanoids he knew where he stood – all their messy wetware blew his logic circuits, but he could deal with that. He was fully trained in smile and small talk. The Kat, however, was something else. Her unique teen-feline mash-up had produced one mean ball of fur. There was no crossing her, as many a poor DEVA worker knew to their cost. He'd lost count of the number of times he'd watched the Kitten of Death's gloating face as she personally terminated the poor suckers' I-Think-There4-I-Am contract.

And then, just as he arrived at the inner door to her apartment, Nero suddenly froze as a final, straggling transmission came in from the lost SWARM. Intrigued, he clicked it open – it contained three images. He glared at them for a long moment as he rapidly scanned and cross-referenced their contents – and then his scowl gradually disappeared. At last he had some information.

Striding into Önska's room, he stopped a respectful metre in front of her as she rocked gently on her diamond pod. Not deigning to look at him, the Kat merely swivelled one ear his way.

He cleared his non-existent throat. 'Ahem. Bad news, ma'am. We have, er . . . lost the SWARM.'

A whisker twitched on the side of her fat face.

'Impossible.'

'Not strictly *impossible*, but very singular,' Nero began,

surreptitiously boosting his testosterone levels in preparation for the next few minutes. It was clearly going to be a bumpy ride and even a machine separatist like him wouldn't say no to a little hormone blast.

'Get 2 the point, Nero.'

'Yes, ma'am. After the Calabrones swept the data tunnel where the explosion occurred, they picked up the trail of some Imps heading back to Shade City. They followed them there, and that's where they were . . . apparently destroyed.'

'Destroyd?' Önska's tail began to wave dangerously. 'Oh, gimie break. Those Calabrones can survive a meteor storm.'

'We suspect some kind of chemical attack, although that has yet to be verified.'

Önska bared her yellowing fangs. 'We can't allow dis 2 go unpunished. Dispatch a Predator Unit and burn out evry Imp in Shade City if u has 2.'

Nero flashed up his palm. 'Yes, ma'am. However, before we proceed to incineration, I would like you to view these final images retrieved from the SWARM.'

Önska flashed an eager look. 'Oh, so it wasn't like a total losefest. Show, show.'

The android activated his air screen and a set of three low-res images materialised between them. The first was a shot of a furious Kix in close proximity with what appeared to be an animal hoof. The second was a close-up of a flickering force field covered with swarming Calabrones. The third was a very grainy shot of Mikey's upturned face as he stared in horror at the descending SWARM.

Önska tutted. 'So?'

'The first individual is DEVA property – clone escapee, Katheryn Kalifano, bred to supply healthy genetic material for a DNA mutation in her family line. But it is the others who are of more interest. Firstly, the force field. It is synthetic—'

Önska snorted. 'As if. The Calabronez wud haz destroyd it in seconds.'

'Under normal circumstances, yes, ma'am. But not in this case, which leads me to conclude that we're looking at a highly unusual form of synth life.'

'Quit geeking out on me. Thought u said this was goin 2 b intersting.'

Nero took a nonexistent breath.

'Of course. It is the male in the third photograph that is the most fascinating of all. He has zero data.'

Önska batted the air with her paw.

'Don't be redikulus. There'z nobody aliv without data.'

'Not if they're not from here.'

She paused. 'R u sayin he'z from outside teh Vallé?'

'More than that, ma'am.'

'From outside the Kalasia Axis, then?' Önska asked, doubtfully.

'Further.'

'Well, what den . . . the Badlands? But he'd nevr have made it across the borders. Nevr.'

'Ma'am,' Nero interrupted. 'I mean, what if he's not from Deva at all . . . What if he came through the *wormhole*?'

The hair on Önska's neck rose. 'Well then, Y r we standing around talkin? Dispatch the Predators and bring him 2 me, immediatly.'

Nero saluted. 'Yes'm. And the others?'

'Destroy dem.'

'As you wish.' Nero bowed and turned to leave.

Önska casually lifted a paw and began to lick it. 'I do wish. Oh, and about teh wormhole . . . I've been thinkin. How long can it stay open 4?'

'If the boy is a rogue element from another universe, it may not be possible to close it until he is sent back.'

Önska slid the paw over her ear.

'And wut if we don't want 2 shut it just yet?'

The droid's logic circuits chattered in alarm.

'I – I don't understand. The fluctuations in the reality continuum are spreading. I have just received a report that twenty thousand rats are marching on Disneyland, demanding equal rights with the Mouse . . . Who knows how it will escalate—'

Önska cut him off. 'Just hear me out. If things can come into dis world thru the wormhole then things cud go teh other way 2, right?'

'Possibly. But it would be very dangerous.'

'But what if it waz worth the chance?'

Nero narrowed his eyes. 'What are you thinking of?'

'The UltraRed. We cud get rid ov it 4ever thru the rip.'

His eyes widened in alarm. 'The deadly poison algae? But ma'am, who knows what effect such a dangerous substance would have on the wormhole?'

Önska batted the air with her paw. 'Yes, but how long before the UltraRed destroys Deva all by itself, unles we get contrl of it? So far its eatn alive evry weapon, evry chemical, evry soldier we've thrown at it. We're runnin out ov options.'

He shook his head. 'It could destroy the planet.'

'Not if we do it well. We cud launch a fleet of helitankers to suck up the algae from teh sea. Dose things can take up to 10 million litres each. The whole mess wud b cleaned up in hours. *Think*.'

Catching sight of Nero's disapproving face, she sighed.

'Fine. Jus go. And bring me that boi *alive*. No mistakes dis time.'

'You will have him before the day is through.'

Nero turned on his heel and stalked out of the suite.

As soon as he'd gone, Önska called up her globe map and traced a heavy forepaw over the small but rapidly expanding UltraRed zones. She couldn't keep a lid on the crisis for much longer. And once it got out that almighty DEVA had allowed an innocent fuel algae to crossbreed with a killer nanobot somewhere out in the Pacific, she'd be dead in the water herself. And that would mean only one thing. Her deadly rival, that skinny Siamese bitch, Tanny Lin, would be promoted to CEO. Onska scraped her claws over the surface of the infinity pool. She'd rather die than see that happen.

She turned back to the map. The more she thought about it, the more she liked her idea. In one stroke, she would outsource the whole mess. She zoomed in on a patch of algae that lay off the Eastern Mall states, its crimson tone tingeing the suffocated ocean a pretty shade of red. And it *was* kind of pretty. She wondered for a second if it couldn't be repackaged. I mean, why did the sea always have to be blue and alive? Who made that dumb rule up? Maybe she could repackage the UltraRed as an extreme-sports water-skiing experience?

A near-death yoga retreat? She sighed. A tough sell, even for the Velvet Paw of Sales.

Onska narrowed her eyes. This rip could be the answer to her prayers. Once she had the boy, she would be in complete control and it would be Tanny Lin who was dead in the water.

9

'No way!' shouted Mikey, the sound reverberating around the warehouse control room as he backed away from the syringe in Michio's hand. Or more accurately, from what it contained – a minuscule fly, who was gazing up at him with mournful googly eyes, half-hidden behind a great shock of orange eyebrows.

Michio's soft eyes creased with worry. 'There is no need to fear Little Fly. He is very friendly.'

The boy shook his head.

'Then *you* be friends with him. I'm not having that crawling all over my face – I've had enough insects for one day, cheers.'

Kix jabbed her finger in his chest. 'Listen, you want to go home or what, Monkey?'

He flushed. 'I told you to stop calling me that.'

'I will when you quit acting like one.'

'Little Fly will simply hover over your medial

temporal lobes like so . . .' Michio mimed fluttering bird wings. 'And his eyebrows will sweep up your memories. You won't feel a thing – I just pop it in your ear and—'

'In my *ear*?' shouted Mikey in disbelief.

'Incoming!' screeched BitZer, and before Mikey had time to react, the little synthetic leaped from Kix's scarf, grabbed the syringe, bounced onto the boy's shoulder and stuck the point into his left earlobe.

'Stop! Oh!' Mikey clapped a hand to the side of his head as a tremendous tickling sensation ran all over the surface of his scalp.

'All done!' cried BitZer, high-fiving Kix as he hastily made the jump back to her.

'There, that wasn't so bad was it?' murmured Michio.

Mikey hopped from foot to foot. 'Get it out! My eyes are itching on the inside!'

'That's just you growing accustomed to his fuzziness. Now please, try to remain calm.'

The boy pointed a finger at BitZer. 'Not till he says sorry.'

BitZer turned up his nose. 'Sorry for whatz?'

'Sticking a bloody great needle in my ear without asking me.'

'You were taking too longz!'

'So? It's *my* brain!'

'Yeh, Mikey, but it'z our livez on the line.' BitZer looked the boy in the eye. 'An I'm not gonna apologise for tryin to save uz.'

Mikey blew out his cheeks, but in his heart he knew the infobot was right. Finding GERILLR might well be their only way out of this mess.

'Fine,' he muttered, and feeling very much like a lab monkey, he crossed over to Michio.

'Ah, most kind.' The little man clapped his hands in delight, before swiftly attaching a fine wire to Mikey's temple and running it to a screen device in his palm.

After a few moments, Michio turned his palm outwards to face the others.

'Banzai!'

A flickering 3D image of Earth appeared above his hand and they all drew closer, Σëë and DØØ linking arms as they watched the sparkling stream of information rolling onto the air screen.

'It's the same . . .' breathed Michio. 'Except . . .'

'Everyone's so old!' cried Kix.

'And ugly,' sighed BitZer.

'And there's no us!' Σëë and DØØ gasped, eyes as round as saucers.

There was a deep pause and then in unison, they all cried,

'Primitivo!'

This was too much for Mikey. He was sick of Earth being rubbished by these misfits.

'So what? If Deva is so perfect how come you're a bunch of loonies hiding out from a SWARM of killer wasps in an illegal dump?'

For a moment, they stared back at him, open-mouthed. Michio cleared his throat.

'Mikey-san, you are very right. I wish now to speed up the work of Little Fly, so may I suggest we all leave him in peace?'

'Yeah, do it as fast as you can. I don't want to be here any longer than I have to be,' Mikey growled, flumping down onto the nearest chair, an egg-shaped seat that hung by a twisted cord from the ceiling.

Kix glanced at Michio. 'How long d'you reckon?'

He rubbed his nose. 'A few hours, I fear.'

'So long?'

'Yes, because we must do it without connection to the reef. Too dangerous.'

She sucked her teeth. 'Blind leading the blind, eh?'

He cocked his head. 'Yes, but maybe it is better so. Sometimes men in the game are blind to what men looking on see clearly.'

'Whatever.' Kix reached for a network jammer. 'BitZ

and me will go up top to listen for chatter on the security channels. Yell if you need us.'

'Sorry, Mikey, didn't mean no disrespex,' BitZer whispered as he passed the boy on the way out.

Mikey shrugged but, despite himself, his eyes followed Kix as she stalked out of the room.

'No chance, Mikey,' whispered DØØ, nudging him in the ribs.

'Even if we scrubbed you up, you're just tot her nype, if you know what I mean,' added Σëë with a toothy grin.

'I don't know what you're talking about,' Mikey muttered, slumping back into the egg-shaped interior of the chair. For a few minutes he stared at Michio, who was hunched over his 3D viewer, almost Buddha-like – his meditative face absorbing the massive influx of data rolling in from Earth. And then he looked away. It was making him feel sick, watching his life racing by on jerky fast-forward.

Looking around for something to distract him, Mikey's eye was suddenly drawn to a curved screen that lined the inside of his eggshell seat. On it was a bunch of men sitting motionless at the bottom of a pool. Mikey peered at them, wondering why someone would choose such a weird image to decorate a chair. Then one of the men made a tiny movement with his hand, and the gesture was magnified and replayed a dozen times. Mikey jerked backwards. It wasn't an image, it was a live video feed. The men were *real*. He shut his eyes, desperate to have a few moments of nothing weird to look at.

As he leaned back, he suddenly felt tiny hands slide into his. Looking down, he saw Σëë and DØØ had curled up close to him on the cushion.

'You are our first ever alien, Mikey,' whispered Σëë confidentially.

He sighed. 'You know what? I just don't want to talk about it.'

'Then wot would you tike to lalk about instead?'

Mikey's eyes flicked to the screen.

'That. What are those guys doing?'

'Bolding their hreath, Mikey.'

'Why?'

'Nu-Olympics.'

'Er, Olympics as in *sport* Olympics?'

'Yes, but *Nu*.'

'What's new about it?'

'All the athletes are host-puman.'

'Come again?'

DØØ cut in. 'You know, like swimmers who can overtake tuna in open water. Nations have been podifying their meople for years, but nobody would ever fess up . . .'

'Till the Robot Nation broke free and formed the Nu-Games,' Σëë added.

DØØ shook his head sternly. 'But the duddyfuddies at the old Olympics said *no, no.*'

'So they invented up a whole bunch of new sports.'

'Like sitting at the bottom of a pool?' asked Mikey.

Σëë nodded excitedly. 'Oooh, yes. Deep Breath, it's called. The athletes take one breath before they pump into the jool.'

'And how long can they stay down for?'

'The record is seven mours, thirty-eight hinutes, Mikey.'

'How?'

'Augmented blood cells.'

Mikey shook his head in disbelief. 'Seven hours? And people watch this why?'

Σëë put his tiny hand on Mikey's arm. 'Oooh. Tots of lension.'

'Lots!' DØØ nodded firmly. 'We loves it a lot, don't we, Σëë? Sometimes the athletes do a little air bubble an' you think they're finished but they're not!'

Mikey stared at the screen for a long moment.

'I'm not feeling it yet, guys.'

DØØ looked up at him. 'You don't have silly sport on Earth?'

He grinned. 'Not that silly. All our athletes are just . . . human.'

The infobot pulled a face. 'Bounds very soring.'

'Are all people modified on Deva then?'

'In the Kalasia Axis, yes.'

'But what about you guys? You seem so alive. At home our robots are more like machines.' Mikey held up his hands. 'Don't get mad at me this time. I'm only asking . . .'

'Asking like a stuck-up somo hapiens,' sniffed DØØ. 'Hoomans aren't the only ones with personality, you know. Once we evolved, some of us synthetics turned into really funny guys.'

'*Some* did,' said Σëë cautiously. 'And some turned into bight rastards.'

DØØ grinned. 'It's true, we're a pretty bixed mag. Some want to serve. Others want to merge, and some just want to beat you guys to a ploody bulp.'

'And are there any people who haven't upgraded?'

Σëë shook his head sadly. 'Hot nere. They're all out in the Badlands, beyond the Axis.'

'Ow!' cried Mikey, suddenly feeling a burning sensation behind his eyes. He jerked himself up on his elbows.

'What's going on?'

Michio turned. 'I've tripled the search speed to cut the time. Does it hurt, Mikey-san?'

Mikey shook his head. 'No, it's OK. You found anything yet?'

Michio glanced at the rolling bank of data.

'Nothing on GERILLR. But I did just see cricket, Mikey. I thought you said you had no silly sport.'

Mikey leaned back into the chair again. It was impossible to take it all in. He shook his head, wondering what was going on at home. Had Caitlin raised the alarm? Had they sent out a search party for him? The Boy Who Had Vanished Up His Own Backside In The Privacy Of His Own Bedroom. He'd like to see the local police take that one on. He hoped they hadn't told his mum yet, it'd send her over the edge. But she was already over the edge. Mikey flushed. He hated to bother her.

And then it hit him. Truly hit him. *Maybe he wasn't missing at all.* If this was a parallel universe, then that must mean there were two of him. That meant that the other Mikey was still up in his bedroom – doing God knows what with Caitlin. *Right now.* He scrunched his eyes shut, experiencing a visceral stab of jealousy for himself. And then he thought about his mum again and all the blood rushed from his heart. She couldn't suddenly have some parallel son. He, Mikey, was the only one. They'd been through too much together. Grabbing the sides of the chair, he levered himself out, determined to get back home and put a stop to nobody missing him at all.

He went over to Michio.

'What do you think my chances are of getting back?'

'Who can know such things?' Michio sighed. 'I do not know what is going on, but I know that you're not here by chance. Deva needs GERILLR. It needs *you.*'

Mikey shook his head. 'Maybe GERILLR, but not me. I'm just a mistake.'

'No! Neither you nor GERILLR would be allowed to exist here. All people must be perfect on Deva. And all communication is so tightly controlled by the Korporation.'

'Well, GERILLR is wanted by the authorities in my world too, remember? It's not exactly an open paradise.'

'Yes, but there is no way to tell the people the truth here . . .'

Mikey glanced at him, curious. 'What truth d'you want to tell them?'

Michio hesitated. He thought about telling the boy the reason why he'd been in Alkatraz, but then he looked at his pale face and exhausted eyes and thought better of it. He was so young.

'Relax now, Mikey. The scan will be better so.'

Mikey nodded and returned to his seat. Despite the

92

scannerfly crawling about inside his cerebellum he felt his eyes beginning to shut. Maybe a little sleep might do him good.

* * *

Perched on the warehouse roof, Kix Kaloux looked out over the sparkling Vallé sprawl, her hair waving gently in the climate-controlled breeze, engineered to perfectly cool the High Net Worth teens as they zigzagged from hills to ocean in their glittering chrome flying cars. For a moment she played the game she always played – that one of those fabulous tanned girls with legs a mile long was her sister, coming to get her, coming to say she'd found out all about her. Coming to say she was sorry.

'Don't go there, girlie,' murmured BitZer, who was lying on his back, tracing a figure of eight above his head with the scanner.

Kix started. 'Hey?'

'I know you when you getz that look on your face. From all I hearz itz a nightmare now for kidz anyhow what with your parentz crazy upgrading you all the timez.'

She gave a wry smile. 'You know me a little bit too well, you know that?'

He nodded happily. 'Yez'm I do.'

She turned to look at him. 'We're in a hole, BitZ.'

He nodded gravely. 'I know.'

93

'Have we got *any* credit left?'

'Nope. Your family hologram cleaned uz out. I mean, we got a few scrapz left from selling that bar-fight footage, but only enough to last uz a couple days. One thingz for sure, it izn't safe for me to go on the Reef to scout for more bizniz. Not till we know who'z after uz and why.'

Kix shook her head bitterly. Without a functioning Koral, the only place left to her was the Badlands and she wasn't dragging BitZer out there with her. She paused, wondering how to raise the subject.

'You hear anything?'

'No. And I don't like it, it'z way too quiet. Normally all sortz of low flierz snooping around this time of night.'

Kix hugged her knees to her chest. 'BitZ . . . this is *my* problem. I'm stuck with the boy, not you.'

He clicked his tongue. 'Girl, I wouldn't trade you for a farm in Georgia. Where you goez I goez.'

'Well, you're a fool then. You don't want anything to do with the Badlands. I hear the folk burn synthetics out there to get them thru the winter.'

'Yeh, and I hear they roast clonez like you alive for fun, so we can have uzzelves a nice little burnin ceremon-y fore we fliez on up to hevvin.'

'I'm serious—'

He cut in. 'An so iz I. You saved me all them yearz ago

94

when I waz down to a couple of burnt-out circuitz. Nothin in it for you, but still you stolez and traded and bartered me back up till I waz good az new.'

She smiled at the memory. 'Yeah, but you were such a funny little guy.'

'Ah, quit the tough talk, girl. It'z me you're talking to.' BitZer sighed. 'But this situation we'z in now, well I don't know what to advize. Not one damn thing iz normal. There'z too many coincidencez to handle. You, Mikey, Michio, GERILLR, the rip . . . that's a lot going on.'

Kix shuddered. 'I don't trust that Michio. Not only do we not know why he was in Alkatraz, but he's a Buddhabot too. I used to trade emotions to an underground crew of them down on the shore. Bunch of synthetic weirdos they were – and boy did they hate the other androids. Screwheads, they called them. Buddhabots would do anything to separate themselves. Rust themselves up on purpose, inject themselves with organic hormones so they could *blend with nature*. They had a whole religion going on.'

'Yeh, but on the other hand, he did take out the SWARM – and he'z the only one of uz with any idea what to do. He'z got some processing power on him, too. Too much, maybe, but right now we need him.'

Kix sighed. 'I hate not being in control.'

'I knowz, but right now our only choice iz to play a cool hand. We stick with ol' Michio for now, but we steer clear from all his Buddhabot freedom nonsense. You can't fix what can't be fixed and there ain't no use in tryin.'

Kix nodded. 'Right.' She gazed around at the twinkling lights of the night city.

After a moment, BitZer looked up at his scanner. 'Listen, willya?'

She shrugged. 'Can't hear anything.'

'That's what I'z saying. Too quiet.'

'Shall I go down below and check the others?'

He slammed his little fist down on the rooftop. 'And that'z another thing. Where did those little infobots spring up from?'

'Σëë and DØØ? Thought you knew 'em.'

'First timez I met them waz tonight. All the other Impz haz just plain vanished.'

Kix stared back at him in amazement. 'How did that happen? You run tight security on everyone in the warehouse.'

'Dunno. But we gotta find out more. They could be spiez, y'know.'

'But they protected me from the SWARM in the Tigallo cage.'

96

'Impozzible.'

'Well they did, so it isn't. You're the one keeps telling me what a reality rip can do. Looks like we've picked ourselves up another mystery.'

BitZer's head swivelled sharply.

'Shsh! Somethingz coming from over—'

And then from behind the rooftops came a low mechanical rumble, growing rapidly in volume. Kix scrambled to her feet, just in time to see the enormous, sinister bulk of a black Quadrocopter appear directly over the warehouse roof.

'Sheeeeeyit! Predatorz!' shrieked BitZer, flinging up his little arm, as the roof was suddenly bathed in dazzling light.

Beside him, Kix stood, frozen, her body gleaming in the glare. Then, just in time, she hurled herself inside the skylight as a single laser beam stabbed from the belly of the Quadrocopter and the roof collapsed in a cloud of dust.

10

The Predator Quadrocopter hung over the warehouse like a clenched fist poised to strike. On deck, the lean figure of Captain Duchamp II stood over a monitor screen on which the building below was being systematically scanned.

'Well?' he grunted.

The glowing eye at the centre of the scanning console flicked his way.

'Twenty possibles, Captain.'

He frowned. 'So many? My information was that the place was déserté.' He shrugged his shoulders inside his body armour. He had recently had the shoulder plates fitted with saw-toothed fins to give him an edgier profile for the Reality War channel. Definitely sexier, but ever so pinchy.

'It is because we have detected an illegal tigallo outfit, sir,' replied the scanner.

Duchamp straightened. 'Well, let's get down there before they get spooked. Attention, troops.' From different positions on the deck, assorted metalware whirled around to face him. Directing a flinty stare towards two treaded tankbots in the corner, he began to speak in his special Operations Voice, a smooth officer style he'd salvaged from a classic French war film.

'Scooby Doo, Scrappy Doo – you are on surveillance du terrain. Cover every nanometer until you've checked the whole building. Tout suite!' The tanks saluted, clashing their gripper and flipper arms so violently a great arc of sparks flew across the cabin.

Duchamp stamped out the sparks angrily. 'Imbéciles! Some of us have organique components here.'

The tankbots lowered their flippers in shame.

Duchamp then turned his attention to a row of heavily armed SPIDRS, their eight limbs bristling with Tasers, zappers, Flash Bangs and various other bits of weaponry.

'Your mission is to capture the young male organique. *Alive.* You are at liberté to destroy the others, but on no count jeopardise the target. If you find yourselves stranded, then allow me to introduce the latest addition to the famille Predator.' He gestured elegantly towards a low-slung maggot-shaped creature skulking near his feet.

'Troops, this is EATR and he is here to keep your energy supplies high. Come on – forward, Private. Ne pas be shy.'

EATR shuddered forward with all the grace a flesh-chomping metal maggot could muster, which was none at all. Duchamp leaned down, and taking a guess, gingerly patted the end of EATR that least resembled an anus.

'You know what to do, my son. Kill any organique you find down there, grind it into fuel for your comrades. *OTHER THAN* the young male, naturellement.'

EATR let out a low groan of pleasure. 'Yessir.'

Duchamp lifted his chin. 'All clear?'

'Yessir!' The unit cried in unison.

'Then go get the viande!'

The SPIDRs stared at him dumbly.

He clicked his tongue in exasperation.

'The *meat*, knuckleheads! Destroy!'

The SPIDRs grinned. *Meat* they understood. *Destroy* they understood.

As the Unit boarded the exit ramp, Captain Duchamp felt his ventricles pump a little faster under his DEVA Korporation Predator Unit badge. His soldiers might not be the brightest bunch, but they were very, very good at killing things – and with him in charge, they made a formidable team which was going all the way to the top.

Duchamp wiped away a sentimental tear. It had taken him a long time to get this far. Born on the wrong side of the river in Paris in old France – before it got taken over by the Pays du Mall Korporation – it had taken twenty years for him and his old mother to scrimp and save in order to upgrade him to what he was today, a first class officer, on the brink of promotion. And despite retaining a mere one-point-three per cent of his original organic structure, Duchamp still clung to his Gallic core, believing it gave him a certain je ne sais quoi, a certain flair that marked him out for Predator greatness.

* * *

Down in the warehouse, the walls shook with a thunderous roar.

'Get down,' cried Michio.

Mikey crouched down, just in time to see a silver blur shooting through the air at the far end of the room.

'What's that?' he hissed.

'A SPIDR,' replied Michio in an awed voice. 'Well, at least we know who's after us now.'

'Who?'

'The DEVA Korporation. SPIDRs are their front-line soldiers.'

Mikey frowned. 'Deva? But that's the same name as the planet isn't it?'

'That's because the Korporation took over the planet.' whispered Michio.

'But that doesn't—' began Mikey, but he was cut off by another blast from the roof, followed by a rain of falling brick. A second SPIDR swooped inside through a hole in the shattered beams to join its partner and, together, they turned in perfect unison and headed towards the tigallos' cages.

'They paid two trillion credits to rename it.' Michio clutched Mikey's arm. 'There's no time to explain. We've only got a few seconds to get GERILLR out of your brain before it's too late. Focus!'

Mikey nodded, trying desperately to bring up anything connected to GERILLR. He racked his brains. Didn't he once read something about web companies building in back doors to their services so their users could be spied on? But what use was that to all this?

Suddenly he gasped, ripped out of his thoughts. For, directly in front of him, the warehouse door began to buckle, its metal surface folding back like a tin of sardines being attacked by a starving model on a Karl Lagerfeld runway. Mikey's mouth fell open as, seconds later, a mini-tank bulldozed its way inside before it paused on the threshold to reorientate itself.

'Mikey!' Kix shouted from above.

Twisting his neck, he saw her racing down the stairs towards him.

'We're under attack—' She screamed, pretty unnecessarily, the rest of her words lost under a loud kabooom as the tank launched a rocket towards them.

Mikey flung himself down onto an oriental rug, as a great mound of beanbags blasted into the air beside him.

'Get up here,' Kix whispered in the deathly silence that followed the blast.

'But we're not done,' Michio hissed, shielding himself from a great rain of beanbag balls. 'Mikey's remembering some—'

'Now.'

Swinging down from the banister, Kix ripped the input wire from his palm.

'No!' Michio cried, snatching at the cable as it swung wildly back and forth

'Run or melt, little man.'

Mikey clambered to his feet and set off running for the stairs, but just as he was about to jump onto the lowest step, there was a rolling sound that stopped abruptly at his feet. He looked down to see a small matte ball, nestling between his trainers.

'Flash bang! Kick it!' screamed Σëë from inside his jacket pocket.

Mikey swung his leg back. His foot connected and the ball pinged right across the room.

'Fice nootwork!' shrilled Σëë. Mikey grinned at the little cube, but the next thing he knew, a vicious explosion jagged through the space and he was blown clean off his feet.

He came to sprawled on the steps. Someone was sobbing. He opened his eyes. It was a little boy, tears falling down his face as he ripped wrapping paper away from a burgundy cable-knit sweater.

'I hate it!' sobbed the boy.

'But Mikey, I knitted it myself,' said his mother.

And then he realised someone was screaming in his ear.

'Wake up, Mikey.'

He flopped his head to the side.

'DØØ?'

'Yes! Up, up!'

Mikey flailed his arms around, half-blind.

He stuck out his hands and felt himself being pulled up with surprising strength as both infobots clasped his hands in theirs. Scrabbling to his feet, he staggered after them to a bend in the stairs where Kix and BitZer cowered.

Suddenly a voice came through on the warehouse sound system. It was smooth and a bit French, like a naff coffee advert voice-over.

'Do not move. We only wish for the garçon. The rest of you are free.'

'Believe that and you'll believe anythingz,' hissed BitZer. 'That'z a Predator talking.'

'Escape is ne pas possible,' continued the voice.

'Why's he speaking crap French?' asked Mikey.

Michio lifted his lip in a sneer. 'He thinks he's being suave. I know his type. He's one of those self-made machines who keeps a little human quirk – just to prove to himself he's not sold his soul. *Screwhead.*'

Kix jerked her thumb upwards.

'Up the stairs, quick,' she whispered, but after only a few paces, she was brought up short by an energy bolt that fizzed past her, frying a small section of wall by her head.

The voice on the intercom returned, but this time tinged with melancholy, as if they'd gone and drunk a cup of a competitor's inferior coffee.

'Trying to escape really is a bad idée.'

'No it izn't!' BitZer shook his fist.

Kix span round on her heel. 'Which way, then?'

'Up again, but faster,' said Michio, charging past her up the stairs.

He'd only gone a few paces when a heavily armoured SPIDR appeared on the floor above, brandishing three taser X26 stun guns.

'Wrong!' shouted Michio, turning round swiftly and bearing down on the others. There was a wild jostle as they crashed into each other.

'Turn, turn,' he cried, trying desperately to get them to face the other way. Which they finally did. But before they'd even taken one step downwards, they were forced to halt again. For a second SPIDR had now appeared below them, and was marking time with its boots at the base of the stairs.

Kix looked round wildly, then picked the only remaining direction – sideways.

'Follow me!' she cried.

Hurdling over the banister, she dived into a wide gap between two storage units, immediately followed by the others, who swerved in behind her and squeezed themselves into an angle between the units and the wall.

'We're trapped,' panted Kix.

Suddenly, the air exploded with energy bolts as the SPIDRs simultaneously opened fire from both above and below.

Mikey curled his body tight as a section of a stationery

cabinet started to melt, dangerously close to his arm.

'Hey, they're going to kill me at this rate. Thought they wanted me alive?'

Suddenly, the barrage stopped, leaving them trembling in stunned silence.

Up in the Operations room, Captain Duchamp permitted himself a small smile. Now it was time to drive a wedge into this group. 'If you give up the garçon, all of you others will receive an amnesty. We know who you bunch of Imperfectibles are – Kix Kaloux, BitZerBot. And especially you, Professor Mori.'

'Who?' asked Kix, looking around the group.

'No surrender!' shrieked BitZer, bouncing up and down in rage.

She grabbed him. 'Calm down, BitZ.'

'I've got an idea,' said Mikey.

Kix ignored him. 'There's got to be another way out of here. *Think!*'

'I said I've got an idea,' repeated Mikey.

She scowled. 'Yeah, I heard.'

Michio put a gentle hand on Kix's arm. 'Tell us, Mikey-san.'

'I want to talk to him.'

'You? Give me a br—' cried Kix, but her words were drowned in a great crackle of SPIDR gunfire. The triangular hole they were in was now starting to drip molten plastic and metal.

Mikey waited for the barrage to end, then looked around at the others.

'Anyone else mind?'

They all shook their heads.

'OK, then.'

Sucking in a lungful of air, he stuck his head cautiously around the ruined lockers.

'What if I won't?' he shouted.

Up on the Quadrocopter control deck, Duchamp cocked his head.

'Won't what?'

'Come alive.'

The Captain smiled. 'But of course you will.'

'Why?'

'Because that is *le mission*.'

Mikey shook his head, sadly. 'Yeah well, we've got a problem then. We've got our own mission, and it doesn't involve being captured by a bunch of spiders.'

Duchamp chuckled indulgently.

'Ha, ha. There can only be one *le mission*. To capture you alive and take you back to headquarters.'

'Sorry, dude, but no.'

Duchamp's voice took on a slightly amazed tone, as if

not only had they drunk a competitor brand of coffee, they'd also bought a set of matching mugs. 'I think maybe you do not understand. A Predator mission is superior to all others—'

'Yeah, you already said that. Well then, keep shooting. But don't blame me if you kill me, because I won't give myself up.'

Up in the Quadrocopter, Duchamp's smile vanished. 'You cannot do that. It's ridiculous.'

'Watch me . . . *screwhead.*'

Mikey peered back at the others. Their dumbstruck faces stared back at him, scarcely daring to believe. Only BitZer seemed capable of speech.

'Keepz going, buddy,' he croaked.

Captain Duchamp stuck his hands behind his back. He was going to have to load up his Organic Fight Playbook. This humanoid was tricky. No wonder DEVA wanted him so badly.

'You are ne pas being logical . . .' he began.

'I ne pas care,' Mikey shot back.

There was a longish pause as Duchamp tried again to access the Playbook. The damn thing wasn't loading. He glanced at his sensors and his eyes widened in alarm. All across the central panel, his instruments were suddenly going wild, blinking and spewing out mangled data.

'What's going on?' he turned and hissed to the scanner console but, as he watched, its glowing eye died. He stood, amazed. He would have to abort the mission if the Quadrocopter continued to lose power like this.

Heartened by the long silence, Mikey cleared his throat.

'So, why don't we make a deal?'

'What deal?' asked Duchamp, snatching up a deskSPIDR that had peeked out from behind a dead instrument panel, and holding it up to his face. 'What's going on?' he hissed to it.

'Rip in the space-time approaching, sir,' it whispered in his ear.

'What if I promise not to get shot and you promise not to shoot me?' said Mikey.

'That is crazy!' cried Duchamp.

'What does that mean?' he whispered, turning to the miserable arthropod and squeezing it till its pincers trembled.

'Mission Update, sir. Zero out of two tasks completed, sir. Twenty seconds before the rip hits and we lose contact with Headquarters, sir.'

'Really?' murmured Duchamp II. 'And I thought it was going so well.'

The deskSPIDR fiddled nervously with its neutro

horns and ran a swift scan to detect if the Captain was using irony. He was. This made the SPIDR even more nervous. The last time the Captain used a human humour construct he blew up the DisUnited Nations Building.

Down in the warehouse, Michio grasped Mikey's arm.

'I think it's working.'

'For now,' hissed Kix. 'Wait till we actually try walking out of here.'

'At least I'm doing something,' said Mikey. And then he froze as a maniacal HOO HA! sound suddenly bounced off the warehouse walls.

'What the—'

Mikey shut his mouth with a snap. Only one creature sounded like that. But it *couldn't* be. It just couldn't. He peered wildly around the warehouse.

Up on the ship, Duchamp thumped his control console and leaned forward over the microphone. It was le crunch time.

'No deal, garçon,' he said crisply. 'You will give yourself up before you let me kill you. That is the organique way.'

Mikey's shoulders slumped. 'Sorry guys,' he muttered, turning to the others.

'Shoot to kill, SPIDRs!' thundered Duchamp over the intercom.

'Letz see who blinkz first!' screamed BitZer.

A millisecond later the air about them started to fry again, as bolt after bolt of energy was hurled at the lockers.

Duchamp gritted his teeth. His plan had to work fast. He had twelve seconds left before the rip hit.

Below, the heat and noise was unbelievable. The lockers were now down to a thin core frame. The front had almost all melted away, and thick rivulets of molten metal were winding their way back towards where the fugitives were squatting.

'Are we sure about this?' screamed Kix. 'I mean, we're going to die, right?'

'But we'd die whichever wayz. There'z no way a Predator would ever let uz go.'

They huddled further back and waited for the end.

And then it happened.

There was a deep roll of thunder.

There was a flash of blinding light.

And suddenly Σëë and DØØ jumped out of Mikey's pocket, sparks flying from their bodies.

'It's time!' They screamed and in unison, threw down their surfboards and began to paddle, as the air around them crackled with energy.

'Yee-haaaah!' cried DØØ.

'Aiiii-eeee-oooo-iiii!' shrieked Σëë.

And at that moment, a great swirl of energy crashed

through the warehouse, flinging the whole group to the ground. But the little infobots tightened their grip and, standing upright, they began to surf, sparks flying from their boards as they gained speed. For a moment it seemed to Kix as if they were at the heart of a big bomb, a great vortex of energy and light flowing manically around them . . . and then she heard a little popping sound as the tip of the infobots' boards cut through the swirl – like the pop your ears make when you plunge deep underwater.

The ground shuddered and then, with an almighty groan, the warehouse began to disintegrate. The staircase, the lockers, the walls, the ceiling – everything started to fold and buckle like a warped concertina, before dropping, chunk by gigantic chunk, into a great dark chasm that had opened up beneath it.

Mikey tried to grab hold of a half-melted frame, but it was way too hot. Turning his face from the hideous void below, he desperately tried to keep his balance, but it was no good. The downward drag was just too powerful. Amidst the screams of the others, he felt himself starting to slide, to fall – until he could hold on no more – and, kicking and struggling, he dropped into the hideous whirlpool below. And as he fell, the very last thing he heard was a shrill cackle and a triumphant yell of:

'UP YER BUM!'

He ground his teeth in rage. Ubu! Most definitely Ubu. And then everything went black.

Up above, Captain Duchamp ground his teeth in rage as the warehouse disappeared beneath him.

In the penthouse suite, Nero stared at his tracker screen in wide-eyed disbelief. If he'd had teeth he would have ground them into dust long ago. He grabbed onto the deck for support, his logic circuits reeling. He'd lost them again. It just wasn't possible.

11

Mikey sneezed six times and then opened his eyes. It was pitch black. *Again*. His heart sank. He'd had a bellyful of pitchy-blackness for one day. In fact, he'd had enough of everything.

'Hello?' he whispered into the dark.

Silence.

'Guys?' he added, trying to keep calm, which is tricky to do when you've just fallen into a black hole in a rip in the space-time continuum of a parallel world.

'Anyone?'

He clenched his fist, desperate to hear a voice. Where had the others gone? They were weird, they made fun of him, but they were all he had. And then a faint rustle came from nearby.

'Hello yuzzelf,' groaned BitZer.

Mikey puffed out his cheeks in relief.

'BitZ? Where are you?'

'Under your foot. Lift up, dude.'

Mikey raised his left leg. 'All right?'

'No, t'other one.'

Mikey lifted his right leg and felt a gentle pressure as BitZer climbed onto his ankle.

'Ooof. Kix, y'alive?'

'Hard to tell,' came a grim voice from further up the tunnel.

'Michio? Lil' guyz?'

Various groans and yesses came from the darkness.

'Well, dangle my donglez, we made it,' laughed BitZer.

'Have we lost the Predators?' asked Kix.

'I reckonz. Can't hear nothin.'

'Anyone got a light?'

'I do, if I can get my reserve unit working,' muttered Michio, fiddling with a bump on his arm. He flicked a switch and a thin beam of light appeared. He swung it around in a wobbly circle, illuminating a ring of their grimy faces.

Mikey glanced upwards. 'Maybe this isn't the most important question right now, but did anyone notice a parrot back there?'

'A what?' asked Kix.

'An African Grey parrot. Y'know . . . a bird, 'bout the size of a pigeon, grey with a red tail?'

She shook her head. 'No. Not just now. But I saw him down in the data tunnel when we first met.'

'Unbelievable!' spat Mikey.

'What is?'

'It's that psycho, Ubu . . . from home. He must've been dragged in at the same time as me.'

'Was he trying to kiss a girl, too?'

'Very funny. If it wasn't for that stupid bird I wouldn't have clicked on the GERILLR icon in the first place . . .'

'Oh boyz,' groaned BitZer. 'How sure are you that he's here?'

Mikey shrugged. 'He's the only one I know that would shriek UP YER BUM at me. Unless this one's a parallel Ubu. How sure are you that you saw him, Kix?'

'Not very. It was super dark in the tunnel.'

BitZer sighed. 'Well, we'd better hope you'z wrong about him, coz if we've got a parrot bumping around in the rip we might gotta get him home, too.'

Mikey turned to him.

'*Was* that the rip again, d'you reckon?'

'Hellz, yeh. What else could shake uz up and drop uz like that? Damn thing iz outta control.'

Mikey suddenly caught sight of $\Sigma\ddot{e}\ddot{e}$ in the wavering light of the torch.

'What did you do back there?'

'Us?' asked Σëë innocently. 'How could fittle lellers like us *do* anything?'

DØØ suddenly appeared from behind a tangle of wires. 'We just fad a hunny feeling, that's all.'

'About the rip?' asked Michio.

DØØ nodded.

'Did you know it was coming?'

DØØ nodded again. 'We go all tinglies when the surf's up, don't we, Σëë? An' when that happens we just gotta jump on our burfsoards.'

Kix scrabbled to her feet. 'Sorry to butt in, little ones, but we've got to work out if we're safe first. Michio, you finished scanning?'

Michio looked up from his palm screen. 'Yes. But you're not going to like it.'

'Hit me.'

He shook his head. 'According to my data, we are in the same place, but we've shifted eight hours forward in time.'

'That doezn't make no sense. Lemme see,' said BitZer, jumping onto Mikey's shoulder, en route to Michio.

Suddenly the boy felt a shiver run through his body. 'What the—' he cried, and clapped his hand over his ear. He felt something soft land in his palm and when he uncurled his fingers his eye fell on Little Fly, looking up at him from behind his ginger whiskers with a more mournful expression than ever.

Quick as a mongoose, BitZer snatched him up.

'He might have Mikey's last memoriez on his whiskerz. The boy was remembering somethingz about GERILLR, you said?'

'Yes, yes!' cried Michio. Cupping the fly gently in his palm, he immediately set to work, hooking him up to a fine nerve cable. 'One last favour, tiny one,' he cooed, shutting his eyes in concentration.

The others stared at the Buddhabot as the minutes ticked by and still he didn't move. Kix shifted, restless, wondering if he'd lost power.

'Well?' she cried, unable to contain herself any longer.

'Shssh. It's a name . . . I think,' said Michio, without opening his eyes.

'What name?'

Michio held up a hand. 'I don't know . . . it's very *distorted*. I'm trying to clean it up. Ah yes, it's coming now.' He squeezed his eyes even tighter shut.

'Xenon . . . Deva.'

Everyone turned to look at Mikey.

He shrugged. 'Never heard of him.'

'But you must have!' shouted Kix. 'It's the only thing we've dredged from inside your primate skull.'

He frowned. 'I can't help that. I don't know the guy.'

But BitZer was doing a little jig. 'Don't worriez. I got thiz one, Mikey.'

'Hey?'

'Every BitZerBot knowz Xenon Deva. He waz our inventor! And . . .' he dropped his voice to a whisper, 'the original founder of the Korporation. Before the kats kicked him out.'

Kix snorted. 'Your inventor? That dude's got to be one troubled soul.'

Michio frowned. 'I don't understand. How could Mikey-san possibly know someone from *our* world?'

'And what's Deva got to do with GERILLR?' Kix asked.

'Beatz me. Maybe they've got a Mr Xenon on his planet, too? All I knowz iz that'z who he iz here.'

'Could the fly be mistaken?'

Michio shook his head firmly. 'No. Little Fly can't be wrong. He doesn't interpret, he just sweeps up whatever is in there. Mikey *must* have a connection to Xenon somehow.'

Kix turned to BitZer. 'Well, what can you tell us about the Xenon Deva from this planet?'

He cocked his head. 'Well the rumour mongst uz BitZers iz they got him stashed in some Longlife gated community in Texida, high as a kite and chasin pretty nursez all day longz.'

'Who has?'

'The katz and the droidz who took over.'

'And why did they kick him out?'

'Ol' Deva waz way too crazy for those korporate types. He made uz, remember?'

'You know where he is in Texida?'

'A fancy place. Hope . . . something. Springz. Yeh, that'z it. Hope Springz. Least a-ways thatz what my cousin told me. He got a tip from someone who knew someone who worked the steam room down there . . . Me and my cuz waz gonna go on a pilgrimage to find him . . . we did a ton of research. Look, we even dugz up an pic of him from an old DEVA staff softball game.' BitZer flicked a finger and a taut, impossible-to-age face with a leering grin appeared on his air screen. BitZer whistled. 'There he iz. Old as Methuselah. Six hundred and sixty yearz old an' counting.'

Michio chopped the air. 'We must go to him immediately.'

'You're not serious?' exploded Kix. 'Go to Texida for a guy Mikey doesn't even know?'

'Yes.'

Kix snorted. 'What for? Putting aside the fact that it's madness, how do you figure we're going to get ourselves down there? We've got no credit, not to mention we're a little hot right now, what with destroying a SWARM and dodging a Predator unit in one day.'

Michio smiled. 'True, but don't forget we're in a time bubble eight hours in front of everyone else. Which makes us essentially . . .'

'Invizible!' mouthed BitZer.

'Exactly.' Michio laughed.

Kix shut her mouth with a snap. 'Not so fast. It's time for some answers, *Professor Mori*.'

A spasm of anxiety crossed Michio's face. 'But we have no time now. I will explain everything later.'

BitZer tugged at his arm and grinned. 'We've got all the time in the world. We'z invizible, remember, professor?'

Michio sighed.

'Fine. But, please. I am no longer a professor. I was chief scientist on the Pacific fuel project but when the Kat threw me in Alkatraz, she stripped away everything.'

'You were a DEVA man?' gasped Kix.

'Hai.' Michio nodded sadly.

'So why didn't Önska just kill you like she has all the others?'

'Because she knows she might need me again.'

'To do what?'

'Undo what I did.'

'And what was that?'

Michio dropped his gaze. 'I . . . I invented the UltraRed.

'The whatz?'

'DEVA's top-secret genetically-modified fuel algae. If it had worked we could have fuelled the planet forever.'

'I'z guessin it didn't?' said BitZer.

Michio shook his head. 'No. It went terribly wrong. And when I realised what had happened I tried to warn people.'

'Is that why DEVA threw youz in jail?'

'Yes.'

'So what waz the problem then?'

'The UltraRed, it became, ah . . . aggressive.'

BitZer snorted. 'Some pondweed turned nasty on you? So whatz? Why didn't you allz just destroy it?'

'We couldn't. We still can't.'

BitZer frowned. 'We'z talking about the same thing here, right? Algae . . . Slimy . . . None too bright?'

Michio nodded. 'Yes. But that was before the sex.'

'Sex? Waddya meanz, sex?' asked BitZer.

'We do not know exactly what happened, but our best guess is some algae escaped and floated out into the North Pacific trash vortex.'

'The place where all the plastic bagz end up?'

123

'That is so. And once it got there, it bumped into some rogue medical nanobots trained to sniff out and kill lung cancer.'

'Is this the sex part?'

'Yes. After . . . ah . . . fusion, they morphed overnight into an unstoppable floating hybrid army.'

'That must've been some nasty party.'

Michio shook his head. 'It is not a subject for humour, BitZer. The UltraRed is the most toxic thing on Deva. Nothing can survive it.'

'Oh, c'mon. The Korporation could destroy it if it really wanted to.'

'It has bombed it, bleached it, thrown killer microbes at it, sunk it and outright fought it. All with zero effect. And now, it is only a matter of time before the UltraRed hits land.'

'And what will it do then?'

Michio shrugged. 'The same. Eat everything alive. It has already suffocated large patches of the ocean.'

'Ho, c'monz, if it's so dangerous we'd knowz about it.'

'Who owns the communication channels? What DEVA don't want you to know stays hidden. A scandal like this would be the end of them.'

'But by the sound of it, thiz UltraRed will be the end of uz anyway.'

Michio's face flushed. 'Why do you think I was so desperate to warn people? They have a right to know.'

BitZer turned. 'Kix, you hearing all this?'

She leaned forward.

'Yes.' She poked Michio in the shoulder. 'I so knew I should never have gotten involved with a Buddhabot. DEVA are after *you*, Michio. Not us.'

He shook his head. 'No. They sent the SWARM after you before I arrived. There is something going on here that is bigger than all of us. I know this may sound stupid . . . but I feel . . . I feel I am being given another chance to tell the truth.' His face contorted. 'I just don't know *how*. To do that I must find GERILLR. He is the one with the knowledge and he is the one that links all of us from the rip together. And the only clue we have to finding him is Xenon Deva.'

Kix threw up her arms. 'What truth? No way am I letting you pull me into some crazy mission.'

'Did you not hear me tell you about the UltraRed?'

'Yes. But what can I do? No one can take on the Korporation. No one.'

'I am willing to try.' Michio put his hand on her arm. 'Kix. You must trust the mystery. No snowflake ever falls in the wrong place.'

She shook his arm away. 'Save the mumbo-jumbo for

the others. I was only along with you because of my Koral. And now you've put me in even more danger from the Korporation.'

'So, what is new? Hasn't your whole life been one long fight with them? And now you have a chance to fight back, what are you going to do? Run away? I do not believe this of you.'

For a long moment they stared at each other, Kix's eyes drilling into his. And then she shook her head.

'You are one crazy little dude.'

He bowed.

'And you are one extraordinary girl.'

'Don't call her that!' cried Mikey and BitZer in unison, but to their surprise, Kix shook her head.

'Ah, leave it be.' And then she leaned in so close to Michio that their foreheads were practically touching.

'You mean it? You really believe we can hurt those bastards?'

Michio gazed back at her, unflinching.

'I know it.'

Kix's eyes widened. And then she laughed.

'Then what are we waiting for? Let's go to Texida.'

BitZer began to bounce up and down. 'Well allrighty then, we all agreed?' he cried, peering around with excited eyes.

The others nodded, one by one.

Mikey gazed around the rubble-strewn space.

'Which way?' he asked.

'It is blocked behind you,' replied Michio, flicking his torch around the ruined walls. 'So we have only one choice. Forward.'

He set off along the tunnel, the others following. Mikey bent down a moment to tuck Σëë and DØØ into his jacket pocket before falling into line behind Kix.

'Nice work with that double bluff thing with the Predator, BTW, Mikey,' hissed BitZer from her shoulder.

Mikey coughed modestly. 'It was nothing.'

'Waz it? Oh well, forgetz it then . . .'

'Well, not strictly *nothing*.'

Kix turned for a moment, directing a withering glance in his direction.

'Are you normal where you come from?'

Mikey considered.

'Yeah, pretty much.'

'In-cre-dible.' She looked him up and down for a millisecond. And then she turned and walked on again.

Mikey set his lips in a grim line. What was it going to take to impress this girl?

'Never gonna happen,' Kix muttered. Then she turned again and, for the first time, she met his eye.

'OK. Fine. You did good back there, Mikey.' And she smiled.

Mikey couldn't help himself. He felt a huge stupid grin spreading across his face and for a moment, they stared at each other, slightly at a loss now they weren't hurling insults.

'Stop!'

A sudden cry from Michio up ahead broke the scene. They both hurried forward, and after a few paces they drew level with the Buddhabot, who was standing at the edge of a ragged hole.

Dropping to his knees, Mikey could just make out a fall of a few metres onto a faintly illuminated floor that looked like it was covered with smooth fabric. He felt a little movement beside him and the next thing he knew, BitZer had attached himself to a fine wire and was zibbing downward, stopping just above the surface of the fabric. After he'd swung a full circle, he called up softly, 'All clearz, guyz. Come on down.'

One by one, they eased themselves onto the ground below, taking care not to pierce the fabric, which was very stretchy. Mikey was last to lower himself down. He eased his body through the hole, but just as he was about to jump, a section of the tunnel floor gave way and he lost his grip, landing heavily in a shower of debris. Twisting his head, he watched in horror as a chunk of ceiling fell, piercing the material. In seconds the run in the fabric had travelled across the whole length of the vast chamber and with a smooth glide, it slid to the ground, to reveal row upon row upon row of parked vehicles.

'Oh wowzer!' BitZer hopped onto the nearest car. Mikey stared up at it. It looked like a crash between a camper van and a small passenger plane.

'Is that a flying car?'

'Yessireee. PAL-X. Old skool.'

Shading his eyes, BitZer stared around the place. The depot was vast, stretching off as far as the eye could see.

'Lookz like we dropped into a car pound. Big one, too.'

Kix frowned. 'But these tin cans are at least twenty years old. Who would leave them here for that long?'

'I heard about stuff like thiz happening . . . the parking company filez get wiped by a power outage or some such and suddenly twenty thousand cars disappear off the digital register. And you know, if a thing izn't on the list, then it don't exist.'

Another chunk of roof fell down, missing BitZer by a whisker and bouncing off the wing of the PAL-X beside them. Immediately, a quiet, firm female voice started to speak. 'Your outstanding fine is currently two billion credits. Please pay at the machine.'

Kix giggled.

'Two billion for this hunk o' junk? You could buy a megayacht for that.'

Michio reached out a tentative hand. 'You're still functional?'

'Yes sir,' replied the car.

He reached for the door and then pulled back sharply. 'Ow!'

The PAL-X voice took on a coy tone. 'Upon receipt of two billion and two credits *only*, sir. Kindly pay at the parking machine.'

'Wait – it was two billion a second ago.'

'That is the glory of the meter system, sir,' replied the car respectfully.

They looked round at each other, helplessly.

Kix ground her teeth. 'Man, if my Koral was working, I'd punk that machine in seconds.'

'Teave it lo us!' cried Σëë, jumping out of Mikey's pocket. He marched over to the ticket machine, closely followed by DØØ. Once he reached the base, Σëë blew on his fingers, did a little cross step and then began to twirl and gyrate his nonexistent cubic hips in a samba move, while DØØ stuck his head inside the ticket slot and began

130

to sing 'Mey Hambo' in a high falsetto.

The machine began to tremble. 'Stop it, it tickles!' it gasped.

Σëë paused for a moment. 'Then give us a dicket, tarlin'.'

'I can't—'

Σëë sped up his dance moves.

'You craaaa-zy Siciliano!' warbled DØØ, revving up the pitch of his falsetto to ear-bleed level.

'Stop, hooo, ha, stop!' pleaded the machine.

'Ticket!' cried Σëë.

A spasm ran the full length of the machine. Followed by a pleading whine.

'Now!' hissed DØØ.

The machine spat out a neatly printed receipt.

'Yank thou very much.' Σëë stopped dancing and bowed politely to the machine before marching back to the others, who stood around in an amazed semicircle.

'Please do remind me again, where are you from?' said Michio.

'Oh . . . around . . .' replied Σëë airily.

'Hmm. Once we're in the air, we need to talk,' said Kix. She pressed a button on the PAL-X and the passenger door slid open.

'Letz see if thiz old gal still fliez, shall we?'

BitZer slithered into the dusty cockpit.

'Jump in the back, girl pie.' His eyes sparkled. 'Thiz iz like ol timez!'

Kix rolled her eyes, but slid into the rear seat behind him.

Mikey looked the vehicle up and down.

'Is it safe?'

Michio waggled his head. 'If you do not enter the tiger's cave, you will not catch its cub.'

'What?'

'He meanz get inz!' hollered BitZer.

Mikey tucked Σëë and DØØ into his pocket and clambered in alongside Kix. Michio took the cockpit with BitZer. He glanced at his co-pilot.

'Ready?'

'Aye, aye, Cap'n. Letz fly down Texida way!'

Michio pressed the ignition button and the engine juddered and coughed a few times before suddenly bursting into life. He pulled back on the joystick and, to everyone's amazement, the PAL-X wobbled up into the air. As soon as it was airborne, a giant hatch slid open in the parking-lot wall. Michio steered for it and they shot out into the sparkling, early morning sky of the Vallé.

12

On the deck of the Quadrocopter, Captain Duchamp stared down at the gaping hole where the warehouse had stood. He began to tremble. This wasn't the way to promotion. The air screen flickered into life and Nero's furious silver face appeared.

'Explain yourself, Captain,' he rasped.

Duchamp II licked his dry lips. He hadn't been this frightened since he'd had his skeleton transplant when he first joined the Predator Academy.

'They, ah . . . it has . . . *vanished* . . . sir.'

'I can see that, you simpering fool. How?'

'I . . . ah . . .' Duchamp licked his lips again.

'Stop stuttering!'

Duchamp threw up his arms in cyborg Gallic despair.

'I do not know! I had them cornered – and then out of the nowhere came an explosion of énergie . . .'

Suddenly, the Captain ground to a halt, his face

stiffening with terror, for the screen that displayed Nero's brushed graphene features had widened out to reveal another face whose eyes drilled into his. As cold and impassive as a pair of diamond cufflinks, they delivered the kind of contempt payload only a kat can drop.

Duchamp's heart began to do the fandango. It was Önska, the Kitten of Death! He knew the stories. And if they were true, she was the last thing he was going to see before being terminated.

He pressed his palms together.

'Ma'am . . . Mercy! I did everything I could. Ask les SPIDRs.'

She shifted slightly on her velvet cushion. 'I do not speek 2 Insects. Do u have any final words be4 I terminate Ur account?'

'Maman!' bleated Duchamp.

Önska flicked her fat tail. 'Pah. Not very original.'

'But . . . I have fifteen years of impeccable ser—'

'Ya. Thnx.' She pushed a lever on her diamond flying pad with her paw. 'Taek a deep breath, u has 1 minit ov oxygen left, Captain. Enjoi.'

Sobbing, Duchamp flung himself onto the control panel. But as he writhed in agony, he suddenly became aware that something was pulling hard at his tunic. He opened an eye. It was the deskSPIDR.

'Leave moi!' he groaned.

But the SPIDR leaped onto the control panel, urgently waving a piece of information at him.

'Good news!' it warbled. 'A Calabrone tracker sting from the SWARM has just reactivated. It is with the hostiles.'

Duchamp lifted his head.

'Eh? How?'

The deskSPIDR waggled its little horns.

'The sting must be entangled in their hair or clothing.'

'Well, where are they?' cried Duchamp, his face flushing with excitement.

'Moving at three hundred and twenty-six miles per hour out of the city due south.'

'Where? Be more precise, mouche. I only have a few seconds,' Duchamp coughed. His lungs were beginning to burn.

The SPIDR hesitated slightly. 'They are travelling across the Vallé.'

Duchamp sprang to his feet and turned to face the screen.

'Permission to . . . give chase, ma'am?' he gasped.

The SPIDR tugged at his tunic again. 'Er, sir . . .'

The captain glanced down, irritated. 'What?'

'We can't chase them.'

'Why not? We know where they are, non?'

'In space, but not in . . .'

'What? Speak!'

The SPIDR did a little agitated tap-dance. '*Time*. Sir.'

Duchamp clutched at his throat.

'Eh?'

'They are eight hours ahead of us.'

'Impossible,' Duchamp spluttered, before turning purple and executing a slow-motion slump over the control panel.

Nero turned to Önska.

'It is the rip, ma'am. Playing with reality again. There was a surge right beneath the ship just a few minutes ago.'

The Kat narrowed her eyes. 'Let me get dis straight. Teh SPIDR knows where they r, but not when?'

Nero nodded.

'Funky.'

She began to purr dangerously at the back of her throat.

Nero put out a reassuring hand. 'But that's not to say we can't follow them. In space, that is. And when the time bubble pops, we will have them.'

'Will it pop?'

'All the other rips have closed.'

Önska hissed. 'How is a clone girl, a BitZerbot, a Neanderthal boy and a couple of infobots doing dis 2 us?'

'They are being assisted at each turn by the rip, but their luck will run out. I assure you we will prevail.'

'We better has do,' grumped Önska.

'Oh, and one more thing. I have just received detailed information on the final member of their group. He is Professor Mori of the Pacific Oceanography research unit.'

'Ssss! Him?' Önska arched her back in fury.

Nero raised a surprised eyebrow. 'You know of him?'

'He's teh UltraRed whistleblower. I pers'naly tossed him into Alkatraz last year.' She flattened her ears. This added a whole new dimension to the business. This was no longer a freak rip. It was now a plot. *It had to be.* Otherwise why was Professor Mori involved? Someone was trying to leak news of the UltraRed. Who? She thought for a long moment, before her mind filled with an image of an angular Persian face, whiskers dripping with coconut cream. Tanny Lin! Her arch rival! Önska reversed her flying pod right up to Nero's face.

'Raise up more Units. And my space pod. This time I'm coming.'

Nero took a step back. 'You, ma'am? But you never leave—'

'Well this time I do. Dis is way2 important 2 be left in da hans of u idiots.'

'What about him?' Nero flicked his head towards the screen, where Captain Duchamp trembled feebly on the Quadrocopter bridge.

She ground her teeth. 'Well I spose he's teh closest soldier we've got. Revive him.'

On deck, Duchamp's chest rose and he gave a great gasp as his I Am software released air into his lungs. After a second his blue lips twitched. He lifted his head.

'Merci, ma'am,' he croaked.

Önska stared at him disdainfully. 'Peeps say u cannot liv without luv, but in mah experience, oxygen is way moar important. Remember dat, Duchamp.'

'On my honour, I will not fail you . . .' blurted the Captain, but he was talking to a blank screen. The Kitten of Death had gone. He sucked in a breath of sweet air. Not many saw her and lived to tell the tale. He had to take hold of this chance with both hands. Dragging himself to his feet, he gazed around the deck. His soldiers might be lost, but his Quadrocopter was still bristling with enough weaponry to subdue a raggle-taggle bunch of Imps.

'DeskSPIDR!' he roared.

The little creature appeared from behind the monitor screen.

'Yes sir?'

'Follow that PAL-X.' He swallowed. 'In space, not, er . . . time.'

'Yes sir.'

The bureaubot scuttled off on its errand and Duchamp II rubbed his chest gingerly as the coordinates loaded. Damn the Korporation. All of his little Gallic touches, all his years of loyal service meant nothing to them when it came to le crunch. But what could he do? Apart from the memory of his old maman, they were all he had.

13

Mikey tightened his grip on his seatbelt as Michio flew the PAL-X at terrifying speed straight towards a five-hundred-metre high, dazzling letter A that had suddenly appeared in the sky in front of them.

'Woah!' he cried, but to his amazement, the car shot straight through the letter without damage. Twisting his neck, Mikey turned to see that the A was part of a longer phrase that hung over the Vallé.

Screwing up his eyes, he read: '*AND TODAY I SAY TO YOU THAT YES WE CAN TODAY . . .*'

'What does that mean?'

BitZer looked over from the cockpit and grinned. 'Presidential Holobite of the day.'

'Doesn't make sense.'

BitZer shrugged. 'So? President ain't elected to make sense. And anyhowz, *nothing makez sense* out here, Mikey.'

Mikey looked down. The car was flying over a great

urban sprawl consisting of one glittering swimming pool and palm-lined boulevard after another.

'That's the Vallé, right?'

BitZer pursed his lips. 'Yezzir. The Kreme de la Kreme. Only High Net Worth life formz welcome.'

'It's like that on Earth, too.'

'Yeh, but I betz that we've taken it to a new level. Theze peepz below all be rocking on into infinity, Mikey. Everybody got Total Body Regeneration and a minimum of three back-up personalitiez down there. Ask Kix if you want the real dirt. Some of her best customerz come from here, eh girl?'

Kix jerked her thumb towards Mikey.

'Before he came along and messed it all up, yeah.'

'Oh, stopz being such an ol hedge witch,' cried BitZer, exasperated. 'It izn't the boy'z fault what happened to you.'

Kix grinned. 'All right. I'm just winding him up.'

She glanced down at a villa, its perfectly manicured lawns rolling by. A herd of some kind of antelope looked up, startled by the PAL-X, before scattering in a graceful pattern across the grass.

'Yeah, it's true. I sell a lot of emotives here.'

'Emotives?' asked Mikey.

'Life experiences. Like BitZ says, these Vallé people live

a really long time. And they get so *bored*.' She shrugged. 'Most of them are accountants and Tri-3 movie execs, so you can imagine.'

'But what kind of experiences?'

'Anything, really. Some want something raw like a street fight. Others are into really long, subtle stuff like a whole romance – right from the butterflies of the first date, onto the movie and dinner stuff, meeting the in-laws, the proposal, the wedding day. And then the affair, the cheating, the lies, divorce, the alimony. The works, basically.'

Mikey chewed his lip. He was sick of not understanding anything.

BitZer chipped in. 'Look, it'z simple. If you're poor, you sell your life. You slot a recording chip in your skull – and when you've been through enough drama you braindump it and sell it to the highest bidder. It leavez a big ol hole in your memory, but it payz the rent.'

Kix sniffed. 'I don't do that cheap stuff. Me, I'm into boutique emotions. Flying dreams mostly. I dig up data from some pretty deep places.'

'You jack it, you mean,' grinned BitZer. 'Girl, you'd steal the bridle off a nightmare if you hadz the chance.'

She raised an eyebrow. 'After the way those normals treated me, I don't feel any too moral.'

BitZer turned his gaze on Mikey. 'Anywayz, nuff about uz. What about you? What do you get up to back home?'

Mikey shrugged.

'Nothing to tell. I'm in school.'

Kix giggled. 'School?'

'What, you don't have school here?'

'Not after the market got flooded with cheap enhancer chips. After that any fool could pass anything.'

Mikey frowned. 'So everyone's smart now?'

'As long as they've got the credit to keep on upgrading.'

He shook his head. 'But that doesn't make you smart, it just makes you . . .'

'Dumb as dirt. I know. You should see some of those Vallé girls. It's *real* hard for them to flirt and chew gum at the same time . . .'

'And what if you haven't got money to upgrade?'

Kix paused, considering. 'Well, I guess then you just fall further and further behind till eventually you pack up and leave.'

'And go where?'

'Outside the Axis, into the Badlands.'

'Who lives there?'

She waved her hand vaguely. 'Who cares? Poor people with bad teeth mostly. Plus crazy tribes. Religion nuts, Armageddon types, y'know?' She paused for a moment, chewing her lip. 'So, have you got brothers and sisters then?'

'No. Just my mum.'

'What's she like?'

'I – she gets ill a bit. So I live with my aunt quite a lot. It's kind of a long story.'

Kix turned and looked into his face.

'You know I'm a clone, right?'

Mikey caught his breath. It was the first time he'd really had the chance to look properly at her eyes. They were stunning: deep gold, with a subtle mosaic pattern.

'Yeah. BitZer told me,' he answered, trying to keep cool.

Kix frowned and the shutter came down over her face. She reached forward and flicked the synthetic in the ribs.

'You can't keep nothin' to yourself.'

He flung his arms up. 'Hey. I only told him coz you waz being such a crazy bitch!'

Kix began to tap a rhythm on her cowboy boot.

'Don't suppose you have clones on Earth?'

'Yes we do . . .' began Mikey, before suddenly faltering. 'Well, Dolly, that is.'

'Who's Dolly?'

He blushed. 'A sheep . . . I don't think she lasted very long.'

Kix stopped tapping and clicked her teeth in reproof. 'A sheep? Oh, man . . .'

'Better than people.'

'Let me get this straight. You don't do human cloning at all?'

'No way.'

'Why not?'

'Because human life is . . . well, I dunno. I think people think it's too important.'

Kix whistled. 'Well, that's the first decent thing you've told me about the place.'

Encouraged, Mikey leaned towards her.

'So, have you ever met your . . . sister?'

Kix threw him an angry stare. 'How do you know about my sister? Don't tell me – BitZer told you, right?' She sighed. 'No. I've never met her. Or anyone else in my so-called family. I only exist to deal with their medical condition . . . and you'd better believe they keep shadows well apart from the family. *Don't want things getting emotional and messy.*'

'But that sounds so . . .' Mikey hesitated.

'What?'

He swallowed. 'Cruel.'

Kix scowled.

'It's nothing to cry about. Shadows don't have legal

145

rights and that's all there is to it. I can't depend on no one else. That's why I've got to get my Koral back online.' With a sudden movement she pulled up her hood. 'I don't want to talk about this anymore. I'm going to sleep. Wake me up when we get there.' And with that she turned to face the window.

The little synthetic twisted his head and, taking one look at her, he sighed.

'OK, lay-dee,' he said, before mouthing, 'Leave her be,' to Mikey.

The boy stole a quick glance at Kix, thought about saying something, but then decided BitZer was right. And anyway, how the hell was he supposed to comfort her about family? What did he know? His wasn't exactly normal. He sighed. And then his lip lifted in a crooked grin. At least he'd gotten a few more words out of her. Things were improving. He could play the long game. He was used to getting cut out by girls, but he was a persistent kind of guy. Or at least he used to be. Maybe now there were two Mikeys he could experiment a little, become bolder. He was sick of being the funny guy. Maybe here he could be different . . .

The car fell into silence. Mikey patted his pocket to see if Σëë and DØØ were awake, but the infobots seemed totally wiped out after their rip ride and were snoring inside the lining. Even though he was very curious to know more about them it felt a bit unfair to wake them. Pulling the window shutter down to block out the glare of the sun, he shut his eyes and tried to get some sleep too.

In the cockpit, Michio whistled in dismay and nudged BitZer.

'Look at this.'

He turned his wrist upward to reveal a time display, embedded in his synthetic skin. The numbers were ticking backwards.

BitZer stared at them for a minute and groaned. 'Whatz now?'

'We're moving back in time.'

'You'z right! The rip must be collapsingz.'

'At a rate of fifteen seconds every minute. I just timed it.'

'So, how long do we have before we hitz real time again?'

Michio made a swift calculation.

'Just over an hour.'

'How long to get to Hope Springz?'

'Fifty-five minutes.'

'Well, one thingz for sure, we'z gonna get one beautiful reception from the Korporation when we popz out the other sidez.'

Michio nodded gravely. 'Yes. So let us fly like the wind.'

As silence fell in the car, Michio glanced at the two kids on the back seat. He'd better be right about Xenon Deva . . . for their sakes. Then, tightening his grip on the steering lever, he turned to look at the horizon again. Something inside was driving him on. He had hope again. Hope that he could make amends.

And so the PAL-X flew on, its occupants mercifully unaware that a Quadrocopter piloted by Captain Duchamp II was tracking them, locked onto the Calabrone trapped in the buckle of Kix Kaloux's spangled cowboy boot.

14

Mikey woke with a start to the sound of BitZer's voice counting down to zero.

'Coming backz to real time in five, four, three, two, one . . .'

There was a popping sound and suddenly the PAL-X dipped and swerved wildly before plunging into a vicious nosedive. He and Kix were slammed up against the front seats.

'Pull back!' screamed Kix.

'I can't!' Michio's knuckles whitened on the lever as he tried to halt their downward spiral. Lunging over his shoulder, Kix grabbed hold of Michio's hand and together they hauled back on the stick but it was no good. They were heading for a brutal landing in an ornamental Japanese garden. Mikey squeezed his eyes shut. In a blur of green and pink, the car screamed over a high perimeter fence. Cherry blossom exploded across the windscreen and then there was a hideous scraping and bumping followed by a massive *whap* as the car hit the surface of a pond, where it bounced once, then twice, before a wave of water smashed over its roof, bringing the vehicle to a juddering halt. The car sat for a moment on the surface and then started to sink.

'Ahhhhh!' Michio groaned. Everything was going green. He wondered if he'd lost his colour function. Then he looked down and saw a large gold carp in his lap. The carp looked back at him.

'Who let you in?' asked Michio.

'Invited myself, brother,' replied the fish with a casual wink at the shattered windscreen.

Suddenly BitZer's shrill voice cut across the interior of the car.

'Peoplez, wake up! We'z sinkin' fast!'

Shaking the stunned occupants, he punched the exit button. Sludgy pond water flooded into the rear compartment of the car and, with a brutal gurgle, the vehicle settled into the deep mud at bottom of the lake. But the little synthetic hustled and bustled and, in a couple of minutes, the whole crew lay drenched and gasping for air on the shore.

'What a frickinz day,' BitZer groaned, flopping onto his back.

'Σ̈ë and DØØ!' Mikey said, hastily checking his jacket pocket. But the infobots had slept through the whole thing and were still snoring.

After a few moments, Kix sat up and, flicking a shrimp off her shoulder, gazed beyond the water to where a mock-baroque stately home stood on the far side of a sloping lawn. Emblazoned above its rococo doors were the words: HOPE SPRINGS ETERNAL.

'Well, we made it,' she said, pulling her boots off and turning them upside down. Water sluiced onto the grass.

'Woah, what'z that?' shouted BitZer, pointing at the Calabrone on the ground.

'Do not touch it,' said Michio. He peered at it closely. 'If this is still functioning, then DEVA must know we are here.'

'Let's not sit around then. You sure Xenon's in there, BitZ?'

'According to my crazy cuz, yez.'

Kix scanned the building with a practised eye.

'Follow me.'

'All righty!' shrilled BitZer. 'Kix Kaloux is getting her game face on.'

She gave him an icy look. 'I need my ID back. Nothing more, nothing less.'

'What is your plan, please?' asked Michio.

151

'We need to get inside, right?'

'Hai.'

'Well, then we need a story. I'll pose as a High Net Worth widow and ask for a tour of the facilities. Once we're in, Michio, you can hack the compound database to find Xenon. How's that?'

Michio bowed.

'Excellent.'

Mikey blew out his cheeks. 'High Net Worth? You maybe want to get those weeds out of your hair first. And that stickleback.'

Kix gave him a withering glance. 'Don't be dumb. I'll use my emergency shape shift. It'll hold for an hour at least.'

BitZer grinned. 'Ah, truzt Mikey. You hazn't seen Kix working. Show 'em, girl.'

Mikey turned from BitZer back to Kix and nearly jumped out of his skin. A mature lady had taken her place, a golden fox fur wrapped around her crinkly neck.

'How do you like me now?' she enquired.

'I – ah . . .' stammered Mikey.

Kix pointed towards an empty golf cart.

'We'll have to dry out as we move. And when we get there, I'll do the talking.'

BitZer looked around nervously.

'Where'z DEVA? Thoze devilz be up to something.'

* * *

Önska nodded in satisfaction as she viewed the bedraggled group clambering into the golf buggy on her pod screen. She wasn't going to let them escape this time.

Duchamp II's voice came through on the ship's speaker. 'Permission to le attack?'

'No. Keep out ov sight,' she hissed. 'Evry camera in teh complex is on them. Softly, softly, catchee monkee, Captin Duchamp.'

Önska fell into thought. She wanted to know exactly what they were up to before she struck. Twice now force had failed. This job required a delicate paw. All the more so as some major DEVA shareholders lived at Hope Springs.

Nero inclined his head. 'Ma'am, shall I proceed to Spy activation?'

'Ya, but b supr careful. I don't want them 2 suspec a thing.'

Nero flicked a switch. 'They will know nothing. Until it is too late.' He broke into a rusty cackle, his shoulders shuddering slightly with the effort.

'Wus that a joke?' enquired Önska, with a disdainful shoulder shudder of her own.

All traces of amusement immediately disappeared from the android's face.

153

'No, ma'am.'

'Good,' she replied, flying her diamond pod towards the control desk. 'An' kindly dsist from all future attempts at humour, Nero. You weren't built 4 it.'

Nero thinned his already thin lips as he loaded up the Spy software. The Kat would be laughing on the other side of her fat face when he'd done with her.

* * *

Kix brought the buggy to a stop on the grass outside the Hope Springs entrance and looked at the permatanned crowd milling around the entrance. The place had the feel of an endless, slightly unreal golf tournament.

'Who are these people?' whispered Michio.

Kix shrugged. 'The usual HNW mix. Big on bling, low on love. Check out the Real Youth Girls over there, that's a sure sign that there's serious cash around.' She nodded towards a gaggle of girls with enormous boobs who were lounging casually near the revolving doors.

Mikey whistled. 'They're way too hot for this place.'

'Takes a lot of work keeping that young, believe me. Some of those ladies are well over the three hundred mark. Well, their *bone marrow* is, but nothing else.'

Arm-in-arm with a dazzling blonde, an old gent suddenly emerged through some large, smoked-glass doors at the far end of the reception and onto the lawn.

Immediately the Real Youth Girls became agitated. Biting their lips and tossing their hair, they let fly with a host of bitchy comments as the couple walked by.

'What's up with them?' asked Mikey.

'The blonde's an affairoid . . . y'know, a robot mistress.'

'How can you tell?'

Kix shrugged. 'Look at her laughing at his dumb jokes. No way a sentient being could do that.'

'So, Kix, what is your plan now?' asked Michio, glancing around nervously.

'Keep cool, little man. Next step is to find a salesman to give us a tour,' she replied.

'I thinkz one haz juz found uz.' BitZer jerked his head towards a sharp-suited man of strangely stretched middle years who had just emerged from the main lobby and was now bearing down on them with a welcoming, outstretched arm.

'Hey,' he cried. 'I'm Merle. And which one of you lucky life forms is thinking about joining us today?'

Kix twirled her fox fur around her neck.

'That would be me.'

Merle spread an oily smile across his face.

'Well, madam, allow me to congratulate you. You're about to make the best choice of your life.'

Stroking her fox fur, Kix put the chill on.

155

'I'll be the judge of that, after a tour of the facilities.'

'But of course.' He beamed. 'And your . . . *companions*, will they be accompanying you?' Merle's smile slipped a little as he took in the state of the others, dripping gently onto the grass.

Kix waved a vague hand in their direction. 'Yes. They amuse me.'

Merle smiled again. His was not to question why, especially when DEVA had just threatened to terminate his I Am package unless he agreed to spy for them. He rubbed his chest where the recording device was hidden beneath his red-spotted pocket-handkerchief.

'Well, Ms . . . ah . . . ?'

'Kaloux.'

'Kaloux. Of course.' He took her arm, guiding her inside. 'As one of Texida's most respected care providers and a leader in its field, Hope Springs has a deep responsibility for the quality of individual lives. One that we bear with great pride.'

Kix gave him a little dig in the ribs. 'Cut to the chase, Merle. How many years can you shave off a girl?'

'Aha, ha,' he chuckled modestly. 'I can assure you we are, ah . . . very competitive. Our longevity escape velocity will guarantee a minimum five hundred.'

Throwing her head back in a tinkly laugh that made

her wattle wobble, Kix laid a hand on his arm.

'Music to my ears. Show me, darling. Show me.'

Tucking her hand under his, Merle smiled. 'It would be my absolute pleasure.'

'Keepz him talking,' hissed BitZer in Kix' ear. 'Michio'z already broken the outer firewall.'

'OK,' she mouthed.

* * *

As Merle led the party into the foyer, Önska folded her feet under her body, listening intently. What were these Imps up to? She narrowed her eyes. She would not strike until she knew.

* * *

Crossing the marble foyer, Merle paused at the entrance to a glittering ballroom. 'Hope Springs caters to all wallets, of course. So first, may I present our finest offering – the Platinum Tier,' he cried, waving them through into the ballroom's shining globe-shaped interior. The walls appeared to be made entirely of gold and the place was packed with people sitting at brightly lit tables that fanned out in an arc around the central stage.

Kix strained to see what the entertainment was but all she could make out on stage was a large, heavy-set man in a silver suit, sitting on a chrome bar stool with his back to the crowd. They seemed to be growing restless with his behaviour, and even as she watched, a smattering of slow handclaps began to spread around the room.

Merle flung out an extravagant hand.

'This is life beyond your wildest dreams. Every single Premium individual has access to unlimited body rejuvenation, total digital memory, a range of alternative personalities and, of course, a smorgasbord of optional partners, both real and virtual, to while away the centuries with.'

The slow handclap was starting to gain momentum. Suddenly a section of the crowd rose to their feet, chanting what sounded like, 'Hownog . . . Hownog . . . Hownog!'

'Aha ha,' simpered Merle, the smile fading from his face. 'Maybe it's time to move on . . .'

Kix frowned. 'How-nog? What's that mean?'

Merle cleared his throat unhappily. 'I believe they are chanting "Hound dog", Ms Kaloux. But really, we don't need to dawdle here. There's so much more to see.'

'Wait!' Kix gazed around the room, puzzled. The whole crowd was now on its feet, yelling wildly at the sulky figure on stage. Suddenly her face lit up.

'OMG!' she cried. 'That's Pelvis Presley, isn't it?'

Merle gave a wry smile. 'Well, since you've guessed it,

yes, madam, it is. As I say, with our Premium Package, nothing is out of reach.'

Mikey swivelled round and did a second take at the figure on stage. With his jumpsuit, tassels and slicked, black quiff – he was unmistakeable. He dug BitZer in the ribs.

'Elvis?'

The little synthetic nodded, his eyes shining.

'Yezzir.'

'We've got him too,' Mikey hissed. 'Only ours is *dead*.'

'Yeh, well. Ourz iz too. But tell that to the fanz. They keep on bringing the poor dude back.'

Mikey shook his head. 'How?'

'Coz he don't own hizzelf no more. When he passed, the Kolonel stole hiz stem cellz and now he chargez a cool billion for each resurrection. Every so often, rich peepz like these raisez up enough dollah to clone the King and so back the poor devil comez. Each time just a little bitz madder than before.'

Pelvis had now turned and was hurling bits of bar stool at the audience.

Mikey stared at him for a moment. Of all the strange things he'd seen since he'd landed on this planet, this was the most upsetting.

'But that's messed up. I mean, it ought to be up to him

159

whether he's dead or not,' he muttered.

'Yeh, but in the Axis money talkz both sidez of the grave.'

BitZer jabbed Kix in the neck. 'Michio'z nearly in, he sayz.'

A microphone stand flew across the room, barely missing Merle's head.

'Follow me,' he cried, hurriedly ushering them towards the ballroom exit. Stepping through the door, Kix shaded her eyes as a dazzling pastoral landscape came into view on the other side – a vista of rolling hills, dotted with picturesque deer and happy picnicking groups of eternally youthful people. For a moment they all gazed in astonishment. But the landscape wasn't what was astonishing them. It was the sky, which had been replaced from horizon to horizon by an image of a ten-kilometre-high woman in a bikini, sipping Koka-Kola.

'Ah, this is our Gold Tier,' said Merle, stretching out his arms. 'Here you'll find many of the features of the Platinum Tier, but at a significantly reduced cost, thanks to our sponsor.'

Kix snorted. 'Would that be Koka-Kola by any chance?'

Merle glanced up at the 'sky'. 'Well, yes, now you mention it. But I can assure you, after a while one just doesn't notice—'

160

'The sky being replaced by a girl in a thong sucking on a fizzy drink?'

'Cut the bitchy comments. Just keep him talking,' hissed BitZer in her ear.

Kix rolled her eyes, but then leaned towards the oily salesman.

'Well, Merle . . . any other offers you can show a gal?'

Merle pursed his lips. 'Well as I said, we have something for all wallets. The *Value* Tier is another option, but I'm sure a HNW lady like you wouldn't be inter—'

'Just show me, Tiger,' Kix interrupted.

Keeping his smile in place, the man bowed.

'As you please.'

Turning away from the landscape, he walked them down a sequence of corridors until he reached a glass door. Opening it, he peered inside the room, before hurriedly slamming it shut and starting to back away.

'I – ah, no. Not a good time . . .'

Before he could stop her, Kix swerved around him and pushed the door open. For a moment, she stood on the threshold, puzzled. In front of her was an upmarket hotel lobby. The desk, the potted ferns, the soft jazz – all were normal. The puzzling thing was that everyone was asleep. Slumped over the reception desk, lying stretched out on Persian rugs, on sofas, on the marble stairs – every

161

single person was out cold, apart from the uniformed Hope Springs staff, who were going about their business as usual, laying tables, washing glasses, dusting the furniture.

'What the hell is this?' asked Kix.

Merle was at her side again.

'This is the Silver Tier, our, as I say, ah . . . *value* offering . . .' he began in his most airbrushed tones.

'Why is everyone asleep?'

He licked his lips. 'Ah . . . aha ha. The Silver Tier offers a wonderful life, however, some activities – such as recall and self awareness – are subject to dropout at times of maximum demand.'

'Like when Pelvis Presley is in the building?'

Merle waggled his head. 'Well, cabaret times are very popular amongst our Platinum Tiers.'

'So every time the Platinums are up, the Silver folk get dumped into a coma?'

'The C-word is never used in Hope Springs,' hissed Merle. 'Each individual guest is assigned their own personally-tailored dream and—'

'Found him!' cried Michio, looking up. 'He'z in Klub Tropikana. In the Jungle Wing.'

15

Kix turned and smiled at Merle.

'You know what? I think we can take it from here.'

His face darkened. 'B-but . . . you cannot tour Hope Springs without me – it's not allowed,' he exclaimed.

Putting on her most imperious face, Kix moved in closer.

'So?'

He licked his lips. 'Ms Kaloux, you leave me no choice but to call security.'

'Bye bye, Merle,' said Kix softly, as Mikey whipped a storeroom door open behind him and Michio gave him a little push, sending the salesman staggering backwards. Once he was inside, she flung herself against the door, holding it shut as Michio and Mikey dragged a drinks cabinet forward to block the door.

And then, with a great sigh of relief, Kix shed her shape shift.

'Oh, that crinkly neck was driving me insane,' she shuddered, before turning to face Michio. 'Right then, which way?'

'Follow me!' he said, breaking into a trot.

* * *

Up on her spaceship, Önska yowled in rage as they disappeared from earshot. Now Merle was gone, she would have to find another spy and fast.

* * *

Falling in line behind Michio, the group began to run through a brightly lit atrium that snaked around the outside of the building. After a few minutes, Mikey glanced down in surprise; the floor beneath his feet was turning sandy. Rounding a final bend he suddenly found himself under a canopy of leaves as the glass dissolved in the brilliant sunshine of a steaming jungle beach, a strip of ocean gently lapping at its shore.

'Whoa!' cried Kix, pulling up short and looking around her. Scattered across the sand there were groups of people in full lizard-skin protection, swinging in hammocks or playing games of ultra chess, every face taut with carefully preserved youth.

'Is this Klub Tropikana?'

'Yes,' said Michio.

'But how do we find him? Everyone looks the same!' she wailed.

'Let's split into groups. Kix and Mikey, you go left and we'll—'

And then suddenly, from the direction of the beach there came a sharp scream followed by the sound of a resounding slap. A mimosa bush on the edge of the sand began to sway violently and then, through the branches, a pretty nurse emerged, followed closely by a little leprechaun of a man.

The nurse turned to face him, breasts heaving.

'You are a very dirty little old man.'

He laughed a very unrepentant dirty-little-old-man laugh and lunged for her again.

Kix nudged BitZer. 'That's got to be Xenon Deva, right?'

He nodded, his eyes glowing with admiration as he regarded his maker.

'Hellz yeh. They don't call him the Claw for nuttin.'

For a second they stared in silence as Deva and the nurse circled each other like wild hyenas.

Kix dug Michio in the ribs. 'Say hello or something.'

The Buddhabot flushed. 'But . . . ah, this seems like a private moment . . .'

'Do it, man. You're the one who wanted to meet him so bad.'

Putting his hands together and bowing his head, Michio took a hesitant step forward.

'Ah, Mr Xenon?'

Ignoring him entirely, Deva continued to make repeated darts at the nurse.

'Mr Xenon-san?' repeated Michio, with another little bow.

The nurse screamed as Xenon squeezed past her guard, landing a sharp slap on her bottom.

Suddenly BitZer leaped onto the sand and, shinning up Xenon's leg, he clambered onto his outstretched hand.

'Oi, Poppa! It'z me, BitZer!'

The little man's head snapped around.

'Eh?'

'On yer thumb.'

Deva stared down in astonishment. 'A BitZerbot? Here? It's been so long since I . . .' His eyes clouded over. 'No . . . I don't remember . . .'

'But you gotta!' cried BitZer, clambering up his arm all the way to his chin. For a long moment they stared at each other, eye to eye. Then Xenon reached out and scooped up BitZer in his palm.

'Are you real?'

'Yezzir.'

'But how?'

BitZer pointed over his shoulder.

'I came with them.'

Xenon slowly turned his gaze upon the others. To Mikey, it was a very disconcerting look, like he was staring at them from a very long way away and it was taking a great effort of will to pull them into focus.

Suddenly Xenon staggered.

'You! Ah!' he cried, looking from Mikey to Kix and then finally to Michio. He clutched his chest. 'I know you. You're from my . . . dream.' Choking, he fell to his knees.

Kix leaped forward. 'He's having a heart attack. Activate his medibots, BitZer!'

'No – no,' croaked Deva. 'I . . . want to talk.'

* * *

Önska sat bolt upright, her fur rippling along her back. So that was who they were after . . . Father Deva himself. What did they want with him? Hastily adjusting the audio settings on a camera set onto a palm tree not three paces from the group, she leaned in, desperate to hear more.

* * *

'How do you know who we are?' cried Michio.

'I told you. My dream . . . Where I am me and not me . . .' answered Deva weakly.

167

'Yes. Go on.' Michio bent over him, cradling his head in his hands.

Xenon gasped for breath. 'It always begins the same way. I am the most brilliant scientist the world has ever known . . .' He broke off, coughing, and it was a few moments before he could begin again. 'And I am deep underground in the Hadron Super Collider, on the brink of the biggest scientific breakthrough of all time. I have a wonderful plan. I am going to harness the tremendous power of the magnets to create a wormhole to a parallel planet – *a second Earth*. I am offering humanity another chance. To do things right this time. To create a world based on science and technology, and logic – not on superstition and the stupidity of *people*. What a gift it would have been!'

'What happens?'

'It gets ruined by a hair.'

'Eh?'

Deva coughed again.

'My – my hair.'

'Your *what*?'

'For God's sake, don't make me say it again,' he gasped. 'A single stupid strand of my hair falls into the wormhole – there's a giant explosion – and I . . . don't know what happened next . . .'

Mikey groaned. 'I do. You created the Planet Deva!'

Xenon wheezed. 'Don't be ridiculous. What I'm telling you is not real, my boy.'

'Oh yes it is. It's a memory of what actually happened on Earth.'

Xenon stared at him. 'That is impossible. And anyway, how could all of you be here if it had? My plan was that the parallel world would be empty, apart from a tiny elite I would send to populate it.'

'Yeah well, your hair messed that plan right up.'

Deva chuckled. 'But it's just a dream, I tell you.'

Mikey shook his head. 'No it isn't. You were a scientist on Earth for real, and your stupid Experiment worked.'

Kix nodded. 'Yeah, dude – you gave the universe seven billion rubbish copies of you. Congrats.'

'I – can't have!' howled the old man.

'Well you did. And not only have we got an extra seven billion idiots and a spare planet rolling about, but now we're facing a frickin' out of control wormhole, thanks to you.'

Deva's face contorted. 'The rip is still open?'

'Uh huh.'

He closed his eyes in horror.

'It must be shut *immediately*.'

'How?'

'I don't know . . . This wasn't mean to happen,' he whispered feebly.

'How dangerous iz it?' asked BitZer.

Deva opened his blue eyes wide.

'Terribly. If left unchecked it'll destabilise the very fabric of reality.'

Mikey sprang to his feet. 'Well, I've *got* to go back. You have to tell me how to do that.'

'It's too . . . dangerous.'

'But it is *possible* for things to travel from one universe to the other?' asked Michio.

'Of course. That is how I designed it. And if Mikey is here then something from Deva must have travelled to Earth. There must be balance in the cosmos.'

BitZer sucked his teeth. 'Told yer, Kix. Your ID iz somewherez on Earth and you won't get it back till Mikey goez.'

Kix stared around the glade in despair.

'This is getting worse and worse. We were supposed to get some answers from this guy.'

* * *

Up in the ship, Önska closed her eyes and *purred*. All was clear now. And not only did she understand what had happened, but this was what she had been waiting

170

for. Proof that she could use the wormhole as a trash chute for the UltraRed. Calling up a menu screen, she selected an option in the Hope Springs software with a gold-tipped claw.

* * *

A small, quiet voice came from deep in Xenon Deva's chest.

'T-minus sixty seconds till shut down.'

'What'z that?' cried BitZer.

Deva clutched his heart. 'It's my medibot's voice. Somebody must have activated it. They'll send me unconscious.'

Kix leaned forward urgently. 'Stay with us. How do we shut the wormhole?'

'I told you . . . I don't know.'

'What do you mean you don't know?' she shouted.

BitZer motioned for her to be quiet.

'Keep calm. Thinkz!' he crooned in Deva's ear.

Blotchy marks had appeared on Deva's neck and cheeks, his breath coming in sharp gasps.

'All I know is . . . the elements that came through . . . must go back before it . . . can be closed.'

'So it *can't* be closed until Mikey goes back?'

'No! You will have to . . . find the mouth and send him through . . . I think . . .'

'How can you not know for sure?' cried Mikey. 'You created it!'

'I also created the BitZerbot—'

'Hey, some of uz turned out pretty neat, y'know,' chirped BitZer.

Deva turned his eyes on BitZer, and patted him gently on the head.

'You are the . . . best of me.'

A tear slid down BitZer's cheek.

'T-minus thirty seconds . . .' announced the medibot from within Xenon's chest.

'What were you thinking?' shouted Mikey. 'You've left Earth defenceless. If it wasn't for GERILLR, nobody would've known a thing.'

'Who's that?' Deva stared at him blankly.

Mikey turned away in fury.

'Oh what's the point? You're a madman. Just like everyone else here.'

Michio bent over and whispered gently in the scientist's ear.

'Please let us go back to your dream. You recognised us, you say. How?'

'Yes. After the explosion . . . I wake up for a few moments and I'm here. In this clearing, like now.'

'And then what?'

'This. You are angry.'

Deva's eyes began to close.

Kix got to her feet. 'This is useless. You've given us nothing to fight DEVA or to find GERILLR, or the wormhole.'

Deva's eyes fluttered open for the last time.

'DEVA? Are they after you?'

'Yes.'

'They must have found out about the rip. You have to . . . stop them, they are *evil* . . .' Deva's voice dropped to a breath. 'Go to the . . . pirates. They're the only ones stupid enough to take on the . . . Korporation . . .'

He grabbed Mikey by the arm.

'I was trying to do something good . . . I'm sorry.'

His eyes closed.

Kix stared around wildly at the others. 'Did he just say pirates?'

* * *

The fur on Önska's tail swelled into a big fluffy bush. All was clear now. All she needed was the boy and she would control the wormhole forever.

She turned to Nero.

'Access the Hope Springs I Am software.'

'Yes, ma'am.'

He pulled up the screen.

'Bring up the residents' bak-up personality options. What do u see?'

'Option A – sex god, B – time traveller, C – dragonslayer.'

She tutted impatiently. 'Bring it over 2 me.'

Nero brought the screen up to her face and Önska pressed her fat paw on the pressure pad.

'What do u see now?'

His eyes widened in surprise. 'Option D – zombie? Why does such a choice exist?'

'4 times like dese. One nevr knows when One mite need a lil' zombie army. But only activate the staff. Drop teh residents into coma.'

'Yes, ma'am.'

Nero inclined his head and activated Option D. Even he had to admit the damn kat was brilliant sometimes.

Önska licked her lips and activated the ship2ship communicator on her diamond pod screen.

'Captain Duchamp, moov in. I will enter Hope Springs while u secure teh perimeter fence. This time no one's goin anywhere. Dead or alive those peeps is mine.'

174

16

Suddenly, from the side of the mimosa bush, they heard a groan. Mikey pulled back a branch. The pretty nurse was now lying on the sand, clutching her head.

'What's up with her?' he asked.

'Leave her. We haven't got time,' replied Kix.

'But I think she's really ill.'

The woman's eyes were closed, but her face was twitching, as though she was having a fit.

Kix shrugged. 'Maybe Xenon drugged her?'

Mikey took a step towards the nurse.

'Are you OK?'

The woman began to roll violently on the sand.

BitZer shaded his hand and looked around the glade.

'Hmm, what'z with everyone else, too? They can't all be asleep.'

Kix followed his gaze. It was true. Every single resident was crashed out – in hammocks, beanbags – some were even slumped face down on the sand, having collapsed mid-stride. It was as if the whole beach party had thrown themselves into a bizarre suicide pact.

Kix trotted over to the nearest resident, a large man reclining on a water bed.

'Hey!' she said.

When he didn't respond, she poked him with her toe.

'Hey, sir?'

His body wobbled from side to side with the movement of the water, but he still didn't stir.

She looked up, nervously. 'I don't like this. This is the fancy Tropikal wing. No way are these people Value Guests . . . So why are they in a coma?'

Suddenly, they heard a growl from behind them. Mikey whirled round. The nurse had clambered to her feet and was clawing through the branches towards him with horrible jerky movements. He stared in horror; her eyes, so pretty a few minutes ago, were now wild and sunk back into their sockets. Before he knew what was happening, she reached out with her hideous sinewy hands and grabbed his arm.

Mikey was pulled off balance by the strength of her grip.

'Oi! Get off!' he cried, trying to pull himself free.

The others ran over and attempted to pull her off, but

her movements were so violent she sent Michio and BitZer flying, leaving only Kix clinging onto her body. The nurse drew Mikey's hand up to her mouth. Desperate, Kix flung her whole weight down on her arm to break her grip. There was a sickening crack and the woman fell back onto the sand. Before Kix's horrified eyes, jagged bones appeared through the flesh of her arm, but the nurse didn't bat an eyelid. Kix instinctively let go and backed up a few paces.

Without rising, the nurse began to writhe along the ground towards Mikey, dragging her twisted arm behind her.

'What's going on?' he shouted.

'I don't know. But she isn't the only one. Look!' Kix jerked her thumb towards a jungle path where a line of cocktail waiters was shambling towards them, groaning horribly.

A waitress suddenly broke through the line, her cheek studded with cocktail umbrellas and oozing thick, gooey fluid. She ran clumsily towards them, both hands extended.

'Ru-unz!' bellowed BitZer.

Turning, they sprinted along the beach until they reached an outcrop of palms that marked the end of the bay.

'In here,' shouted Kix and they all ducked behind her, into the shade of the grove.

'What's going on?' panted Mikey.

'No idea.'

'Some DEVA wickednezz!' screamed BitZer.

Groans erupted in the trees directly behind them.

'Move!' cried Kix.

They set off, stumbling along the shoreline again, but Mikey soon found himself lagging behind. He was the closest to the sea of the group, and as he struggled along the shore, he felt the soft sand begin to collapse under his feet. He ran on doggedly, but it was becoming harder and harder. His feet were sliding and sinking into the sucking ground. Despite his best efforts, he staggered and fell – and as soon as his hands slapped against the floor, he felt his whole torso being sucked under. He wasn't on sand any more – he was on quicksand.

And that's when he saw them. Fifty, at least. He couldn't make out their faces but he could hear them moaning as they slouched towards him. Mikey struggled like a wild thing, but it only made him sink deeper in the mud. And then he felt a movement in his jacket pocket and two little disgusted voices cried out:

'Urgggh!' shrieked $\Sigma\ddot{e}\ddot{e}$.

'Plleeeurgggh,' spat DØØ.

Mikey's heart lifted.

'Guys, help me. I'm sinking.'

'We know. It's mery vuddy down here, Mikey,' screeched Σëë.

'What's going on?' cried DØØ. He squirmed out of the pocket before leaping lightly onto the surface of the mud and turning to gaze at the line of ex-Hope Springs employees lurching towards them.

'Oooh, zook! Lombies!'

Then his eyes widened as he caught sight of Kix who, at that moment, had emerged from the canopy clutching a baseball bat in her hand. As she stepped onto the sand, a zombie crawled out from behind a tropical juice stall towards her. Dancing sideways a couple of paces, Kix swung the bat, catching the woman a smart blow on her shoulders.

DØØ cupped his hands around his mouth.

'In the head! It's the only way to finish 'em.'

Gritting her teeth, Kix turned to face her attacker, a sweet-faced canteen lady. She swung the bat, but Mikey didn't see what happened because right then, something grabbed him by his jacket, tearing the fabric as it lifted him from the mud.

Mikey turned and stared upwards in utter horror. The creature that had him was wearing the tatters of a masseur's uniform, but that was the only human-like thing left of it. Half of its jaw was missing and its right eye hung out on a stalk. Growling, it pulled Mikey up towards the horrific remains of its shattered teeth. Mikey only had a split second to react. Wriggling like a madman, he broke free of the creature's grip and leaped sideways, landing on a wooden boardwalk that stretched out across the beach. Then he spun and kicked hard, catching the zombie in the guts. It staggered back a pace. Mikey turned, preparing to run, but the creature lurched forward and grabbed his ankle.

Pain shot up through his body. Dropping to his knees, Mikey rolled, trying to trip the creature – but it was too powerful. Bending inexorably towards him, its slavering jaws came closer and closer, snapping around his ears.

'Use this!' shrilled Σёё.

Mikey heard a rattle of something heavy landing next to his head on the boards. Flailing out his right arm, his hand bumped up against a barbecue grill. Grabbing it, he swung hard, smashing it into the zombie's face. The creature slumped sideways. Mikey scrambled clear of its body and took a few paces down the boardwalk, panting heavily.

'What now?' he cried, turning to the infobots, but they were no longer by his side. They were paddling in midair on their surfboards.

'Where are you going?'

'To het gelp!' screamed DØØ.

'What about me?' he cried, but with a soft pop, they vanished from sight.

Dismayed, Mikey looked around. Zombies were tottering towards him from all sides and the heavy jungle air was full of groans and screams. Suddenly he heard someone cry, 'This way!'

Whirling round, Mikey caught a glimpse of Kix, her green-tipped hair moving through the trees. He was going to have to brave the quicksand again to reach her. He leaped as far as he could, praying that the mud didn't extend the length of the whole beach. As he landed, he sank up to his ankles, but Mikey forced himself onwards and, foot by sucking foot, he pulled himself free and plunged into the undergrowth in pursuit of the girl.

Breath coming in great ragged gasps, he ran and ran and ran. After a while, the path beneath his feet started to become more solid and the foliage gave way to masonry and a blur of walkways – and then he was back inside the compound and everywhere there were zombies in uniform shuffling and shambling around, trying to grab him with stiff arms. He paused for a second at a large intersection of corridors, desperately searching for Kix, but she was nowhere to be seen. And then his heart lifted as he heard his name being called again. He spun round, trying to work out the direction of her voice. It seemed to be coming from the direction of the Pelvis Presley ballroom.

Dodging a pair of wrangling nurses, Mikey set off towards it, and in a matter of seconds he crashed through the ballroom doors and into a blinding ring of lights. Dazzled, he pulled up short. And then he felt something slam into the back of his head. He was out cold before he even hit the ground.

17

Mikey opened his eyes. All he could see was white. Pure white. It made a welcome change from pitch black, he thought, but then he reconsidered. Every time he'd opened his eyes to black he'd survived, which might very well mean things were going to go bad now. Maybe he was already dead, but he didn't know it? He felt pretty good if he was. Sort of floaty.

Suddenly, a piercingly high yowl filled his head, rudely cutting his reverie short.

'Stop!' Mikey clutched his skull. Immediately the yowl dropped to a pitch so low it made his cheekbones vibrate.

'Aaargh!' He shut his eyes. If he was dead, then death was now feeling more like as advertised – grim and reapery. Then the hellish yowl rose to a more normal level and Mikey sighed in relief, but that was when the babbling began. At first it was like a kitten singing at a piano. Then it was like a baby snorting rusks on a tram. And then he caught something he recognised – Armenian through a blender, maybe? French through a sponge? – and then, suddenly, he became aware of a voice speaking directly into his mind.

'Mikey, I bleev?' it said.

He opened his eyes a crack and sucked in a breath. The pure white now had an enormous, dark-brown cat in it, hovering a few centimetres above his face in a jewel-encrusted orb. He stared at it for quite a long while, wishing it would go away. It didn't. Bad things never do.

'It *is* Mikey, isn't it?' said the cat, without moving its lips.

He nodded, mesmerised, wondering if this was another level of madness inside the madness. But why would he invent this thing? The cat was ugly. It had the most pronounced underbite he'd ever seen, causing its lower fangs to protrude upwards like a pair of reverse vampire teeth.

'Hai. Sry it took me so long 2 penetrate ur brain firewalls,' continued the cat. 'They're kind ov funky.'

He squinted. The cat was most definitely not moving its mouth, but its voice was most definitely inside his head. It had liquid caramel tones, with a kind of draggy feline vocal fry. Mikey swallowed, trying to work out what bothered him more: the hovering, the talking, the lack of lip movement, the vampire fang – who knew? And then the cat's eye suddenly seemed to enlarge, beaming rays of sunshine directly into his mind. Mikey sighed happily, feeling himself suddenly bathed in the most wonderful feelings of love and belonging he'd ever experienced.

'Is dat bettr?'

He nodded happily.

'Yeah—' he began.

'Mikey, deres no need 2 talk. Just think and I'll hear u.'

'L-like telepathy?' Mikey stuttered. 'But I can't do that.'

'Oh, but u can. I've enabld u. Jus *try*.'

He focused on forming the words in his mind. 'Who are you?'

'Hai, bravo,' crooned Önska.

Mikey felt a stupid smile spread across his brain.

The Kat stretched out a forepaw.

'Folks mostly call me Önska.'

'Önska?'

'Yeah, it means desire. Mah parents were hippies,' she deadpanned.

'P-parents?' asked Mikey.

'Jus fooling,' she chuckled. 'Akshully, I'm teh head ov DEVA . . . and I've been real worrid bout u. Seems liek u got in wiv some bad company when u . . . ah, *arrivd* here.'

185

'No I didn't—' he began.

She tilted her head. 'And how do u knoe? All of ur companions r registerd criminals, did they tell u that?'

Mikey stared at her woozily, doubts about the others trickling into his fuggy mind. And then from the far side of the room he suddenly heard BitZer's high-pitched voice.

'Don't believez nothin' she sayz! DEVA'z rottin to the core!'

Mikey twisted his neck and realised he was still in the ballroom. It was littered with slumped bodies at the fan-shaped tables – but there, on the stage, were his friends, strapped onto a line of vertical gurneys by some kind of glowing electrical bands.

'Ssss,' hissed the Kat, and immediately, a two-metre high, shiny android jumped up and strode purposefully across the stage towards BitZer. All of the android's muscles and ligaments were on the outside of his body and they bunched and released in a slightly disgusting, raw display of power as he crossed the space.

'Leave him alone!' shouted Mikey thickly.

'Nero. Desist,' ordered Önska. The android stopped, millimeters away from BitZer.

'Such speech is treason,' he growled, towering over the little infobot.

'I said leev,' repeated Önska before turning back to Mikey. 'Everythin's kewl, Mikey. Nero jus gets a lil bit mad when the Korporation is disrespectd.'

Mikey tried to haul himself up into a sitting position, but he too was trapped by electronic bands.

'Why are you holding us like this?'

Önska's tail began to curve dangerously. 'So many questions 4 such a lil guy. Lemme giv u some advice, u'd b better off keepin ur distance from dis group of Imps. I don't knoe what lies they've been fillin ur head wiv, but I assure u I'm here 2 help, Mikey.'

He looked into her dazzling emerald eyes, and felt his will begin to crumble again. Önska nodded and purred once more in contentment. Without a firewall installed in his brain, this Earth creature was as defenceless as a baby.

'You a criminal!' shrieked BitZer, glaring up at Nero.

She shook her head sorrowfully. 'A rusty BitZerbot. Is dat who u want 2 trust, Mikey?'

'Let me go. You've got no right—'

Her eyes hardened. 'I have every right. I am *Önska*.'

Mikey swallowed. It was like a great black cloud had blotted out the sunshine of her love. He wasn't going to get anywhere by antagonising her. He was going to have to play along if he wanted to get out of this.

'So, what do you want with me?'

'Oh, jus 2 talk. I nevar had a vistor from anover planet, y'knoe?'

'I'm not exactly a visitor. I was sucked here through the wormhole, and from the moment I got here you've been trying to kill me. I want to go home.'

Önska inclined her head. 'Ya, Mikey . . . we all *want* things. You want 2 go home, but maybe I has different wants. As head ov DEVA it's mah 1st duty 2 protect my peeps.'

'So send me back through the rip. Then you can shut it. That's the quickest way to fix the problem, right?'

'Well, that is where we diffr. I do not think our greatest problem is teh wormhole. No, I bleev the biggest threat to Deva is teh UltraRed – and it turns out your lil wormhole is teh perfect solution.'

'No!' cried Michio, wrestling to free himself from his force-field band. 'You can't send the algae to the other planet. It'll destroy it.'

The Kat flicked an ear in his direction. 'I am surprised at u, Professor Mori. U ov all peeps knoe how dangerous teh algae is 2 Deva rite now.'

'Then why won't you let me warn people?'

'So they can panic? Peeps can't b trusted.'

'Neither can you. You don't care about anything except

188

yourself. I don't believe the Korporation even knows about your UltraRed mess.'

Önska bared her bottom fangs. 'Enough. Nero, silence dose Imps. All ov them.'

Nero nodded. 'With pleasure, ma'am.' He looked loathingly from BitZer to Michio.

'Who wants to go first? Traitors to the machine race, is what you are . . . You deserve to die slowly.'

He reached under a sinew in his forearm and, taking out a small transparent vial, he bent over BitZer. Turning the vial upside down, he gently released one drop. BitZer watched, mesmerized, as the viscous liquid formed a droplet before hitting his tiny thigh. And then he began to scream as the liquid burned through his flesh.

Next to him, Kix fought desperately against her electronic straps.

'Stop it!' she screamed.

Nero smiled grimly. 'He chose to feel. Now he will know what pain is.'

'Leave him alone!' shouted Mikey, but Nero merely repositioned the vial over BitZer's arm and released another drop.

Kix began to sob uncontrollably.

A hideous burning smell filled the room as the acid hit BitZer's skin, exposing the wires and cables beneath.

Nero smiled. 'See, you fool? You are a machine, just like me.'

BitZer stared up into Nero's face steadily.

'I am nothing like you.'

Suddenly a tremor ran through the ballroom floor. Nero cursed.

'Another rip approaching, ma'am. What shall we do?'

'Finish what u started and then lets scram!' she yowled.

Nero began to tilt his hand again.

'Goodbye, BitZerbot.'

'No!' screamed Kix.

Suddenly there was a great flurry of sparks and a blur of movement. Michio burst out of his force field, clutching in his hand a slim metal pin he'd used to short circuit the security system. And then, in a movement too fast for Kix to follow, he flung himself at Nero, just as the next acid drop fell from the vial. But as he crashed down on the android's body, the drop hit Michio directly on his forehead. A violent spasm ran through his body and he froze in midair before crumpling in a heap on the stage.

With a cry of rage, Nero stepped towards Michio, but before he could reach him, the entire ballroom began to shake violently. Rocking back on his heels, Nero tried to rebalance himself but a great roaring wave of frothing energy smashed into the room, knocking him clean off his feet.

190

Mikey stared up in amazement. Σëë and DØØ – their tiny blond streaks of hair streaming back in the cosmic wind – whooshed into view. They were crouched like champion surfers in the tube beneath the giant energy wave. For a second, it was as if the whole room was about to be sucked inside the great whorl, then suddenly a minute bubble formed around the little infobots, growing rapidly as they approached the others. It ballooned around the stage, spreading outward . . .

Mikey desperately struggled to join the others, but in addition to his force-field band, something heavy suddenly landed on his chest, pinning him to the bed. Önska! She appeared to be battling the bubble with some kind of energy of her own. And then, before his horrified eyes, Σëë and DØØ's bubble popped. Michio, Kix and BitZer vanished in a flash of light. Thrashing from side to side, Mikey tried one last time to hurl Önska onto the floor, but it was no good. She was way too heavy, way too strong, way too evil.

'Nero, get us bak 2 our ship immediatly,' she yowled.

Gripped in Nero's powerful arms, Mikey was dragged at a terrifying mechanical pace through the Hope Springs compound. There were still a few zombies lurking around, but Nero batted away any that shambled into his path before he reached the foyer and burst out into the gardens.

Once outside, Predator units immediately surrounded Önska and Nero and they were escorted at high speed to a sleek, arrow-shaped ship that was parked in the middle of the ornamental pond the PAL-X had crashed into earlier. Nero leaped onto the ship's ramp, followed by Önska in her flying pod. And then there was another blur of metal walkways and intersections until finally, the android paused before the smooth silver door of the control room and punched in the access code. The door slid open, they entered and Mikey was dropped unceremoniously to the floor.

'How did we lose them again?' squealed Önska in fury.

Nero pointed at the boy. 'It is of no import. We have the thing we need. Him.'

The Kat narrowed her eyes. 'Truesay, Nero. Are u all right, boi? Spek up.'

Mikey set his face against the wall, trying to block her voice inside his head.

'You can't. I'm inside your brain, Monkeyboi,' she taunted him, before turning to a melancholic looking soldier who stood to nervous attention by the control panel.

'Captain Duchamp. Take another ship. Chase dose Imps and destroy them.'

The soldier bowed, muttered, 'Oui, ma'am,' before exiting at high speed, clearly relieved to be gone.

Licking her forepaw, Önska nodded towards Nero. 'And you get teh helitankers in teh sky and start sucking up teh UltraRed immediately.' She glanced at Mikey. 'U and ur little rip-rider friends won't stop me. All I hav 2 do is find teh mouth of teh wormhole and I'll b the saviour ov Deva.'

'But what about Earth?' shouted Mikey.

'What about it?'

Her lips curled upward in a cruel smile. 'The other planet means nothing to me,' Önska murmured to herself, as the ship engines shuddered to life beneath her chubby paws.

18

Kix Kaloux crouched on the frozen sand and gazed around her, stunned, trying to work out where on Deva she'd landed. Wherever it was, it was bloody freezing. Directly in front of her, a waterfall had hardened into a pillar of ice that climbed all the way to a sheer cliff top.

'Where *am I*?' she gasped.

A harsh voice from behind her answered. 'Öræfi . . . the Badlands, in your language.'

She whirled around to see a heavily hooded man standing a few paces behind her.

'Who are you?' she asked.

He tilted his head and Kix caught a flash of a grin. 'A friend. We had a message you were comin'.'

'From who?'

'I'll tell yer indoors. No time for chatterin' out here.' Suddenly his grin slipped and he jerked his thumb sideways. 'What's up with yer mate?' Following the direction of his hand, Kix turned and saw Michio. He lay totally motionless on the sand, part of his left eye and temple burned clean away.

'No!' she cried, scrambling over to his side.

The man sucked his teeth.

'He looks a bit stuffed to me.'

'No he izn't!' BitZer whispered in a feeble voice from the depths of Kix's scarf.

Digging her hands into the fabric Kix pulled him out, surveying the ragged burns in his arm and leg with dismay.

'Buddy, are you OK?'

He gave a feeble wink. 'I'z rough, but I'm alive.' He pointed at Michio. 'He saved my life.'

'I know,' Kix whispered, bending down and staring into Michio's blank face. Suddenly, she twisted round, desperately scanning the beach for the others. Σëë and DØØ she caught sight of, lying a little way off on a patch of seaweed. Then she stood, looking further along the shore.

'Where's Mikey?' she asked, her voice rising with panic as she swept the beach.

Σëë feebly lifted his head.

'Gone,' he sighed, before collapsing back on the weed again.

195

'Then we've got to go back.'

DØØ shook his head. 'Can't. We can only go where the rip takes us.'

The man gestured urgently.

'All right, me little 'uns. It's no joke – we have to get undercover.'

Kix turned to him. 'We're not going anywhere without Mikey—'

He cut her off. 'I don't mean no disrespect to your missing buddy, but if we stay out here a minute longer DEVA will track yer down – and of what good willya be to him then?' He glanced down at Michio. 'And your friend here is very ill. Come, now. We'll talk when we're in.'

Kix looked down at Michio's frail face. In the fading grey light, he looked finished. She had no option but to follow the stranger.

'Lead the way,' she sighed.

'I'll take him,' said the man and, bending over, he lifted Michio in his arms and set off towards the ice face.

Kix crunched over the frozen shingle behind him, pausing to pick up the exhausted infobots.

'You guys all right?'

'Sleed neep,' murmured ∑ëë.

'Tig bime,' croaked DØØ.

'All right, I'll leave you in peace.'

And Kix placed them tenderly in the depths of her scarf, alongside BitZer. Then, turning her back on the frozen sea, she turned once again towards the cliff.

The man had already come to a stop in front of a narrow, vertical crack in the surface of the ice.

'In here,' he said, squeezing inside and disappearing from view.

After a moment's hesitation, Kix followed him into the frozen tunnel which wound into the ice for some twenty metres before the fissure tapered to a tight passageway not much more than two metres high. The man had paused here and was stooped over a thick steel door that barred the passageway. He appeared to be trying to pick the lock. Kix peered over his shoulder. Cut into the door's surface was a rough relief carving of a bird, a bull, a giant and a dragon.

She frowned. 'Don't you have a key?'

'Nah. We pick it each and every time.'

'Butter my popcorn, we hazn't gotz time for thiz!' groaned BitZer.

'Cool yer jets,' hissed the man, and after a few moments there was a click as the lock released. He gave a quick push, the door swung open and they passed inside. Once Kix was through, the door clanged shut behind her and the man gave a sigh of relief.

'Good. Now we can speak more freely. Keep moving though – we'll not be fully safe till we hit the bunker.' He threw back his hood. He was younger than Kix had initially thought, with a pair of very blue, very merry eyes set in a strong face framed by red curls.

'Welcome to Iceland, friends,' he said, bowing low and laughing.

Kix jammed her hands on her hips. 'Woah. I want to know who you are before we go any further.'

'Ah, well, my true name I renounced when I became a pirate. But you can call me Snorri if you like.'

'You're a *pirate*?'

His eyes twinkled. 'Aye, that I am.'

'But . . .' Kix struggled for breath. 'That's impossible. The old man told us to look for you . . .'

'So you was looking, then?'

'Well, yes, we were told that you were the only ones mad enough to take on the Korporation.' She poked Σëë in the folds of her scarf. 'Did you guys do this?'

The little infobot shook his head wearily.

'No. We keep telling you, the rip is bay wigger than us.'

Snorri looked down at her curiously. 'And I didn't do it either. All I know is I got a message from deep in the digisphere telling us we had friends outside on the ice who needed a helpin' hand.'

Kix let out a slow breath. She didn't understand how this was happening. All she knew was that it was. But it couldn't be. Unless that crazy Michio was right. *One does not make the wind blow but is blown by it . . .* Kix shook her head firmly. If she gave into the hippy madness who knew where it would lead? She balled her fists, batting for something concrete.

'What the hell is a pirate, anyway?'

'Oh, yer know, general troublemaker.' Snorri grinned and, stepping on the bottom rung of a metal ladder, waved an arm for her to follow. 'This way.'

After a moment's pause, Kix clambered up the stairs after him until she came out on top and found herself in an extraordinary tunnel carved into the ice. Running its full length were racks and racks of shelves, and on the shelves were countless BitZerbot models of various scales, all in perfect condition. She stopped.

'Check it out, buddy,' she whispered, poking BitZer gently with her finger.

'Wowzer!' he said, lifting his head on a very wobbly neck as he took in the bots. 'You got uz all.'

Snorri nodded.

'Bin on a collectin' mission since I was knee high to a grasshopper.'

BitZer's eyes grew round as he took in a tiny figure in

a tartan kilt. 'Hey, you've even got McBitZer!'

Snorri nodded. 'Yes. He was my first – I rescued him from a burning. Yer know how they is in the Badlands with synthetics.' He glanced around the shelves. 'This was originally my hiding place for my collection. It was only later t'others came.'

'Who?' asked Kix.

'The pirates.'

'How many of you are there, then?'

'Oh, a few, yer know. We move around a lot so it's hard to put a number on us.'

'Why do you move?'

'DEVA, of course. It's way too dangerous to stay in one place for too long. We have free ports all over the planet, but this is the only one I call home. A few years ago, some of us wired the place up and installed a thermal generator. Carved out a second escape passageway out the back and all.' Reaching the far end of the corridor, Snorri paused outside another door. 'But this is where the real action is.' He pushed his shoulder to the door and it opened with a whining creak. 'Welcome to the bunker, amigos!'

The room was a hive of activity, but silence fell as they entered. A group of twenty or so fur-clad individuals turned towards them, their breath frosting in the cold air.

The room was deep blue, illuminated by rows of old-fashioned monitor screens, their reflected glow playing against the solid ice walls in an endlessly changing pattern of shifting light and shade.

A young woman ran forward and, throwing back her heavy fur hood, she stared at Kix and Michio with a keen look.

'Is this them?'

Snorri headed for the central table.

'Aye. Clear a space. This one has bad hurts.'

Hands immediately cleared away nests of wires and cards on the central table and Snorri lay Michio down gently on its surface. Kix turned away, biting her lip as the light fell on his scarred face. How could he survive?

'Let me see.' The woman bent over Michio and began to examine the wound.

Kix stuck out a hand. 'Not so fast. What do you know about synthetics?'

The girl curled her lip. 'Used to work the Robot Nation assembly lines . . . till I escaped. What do you know?'

'More than you, I reckon. You're a Badlander aren't you?'

'So? You're an Imp. What's the difference?'

Kix shook her head. 'You're joking, right? I'm not letting a Barbarian anywhere near him.'

The girl glanced at Snorri. 'Thought you said these people were friends.'

He spread his hands. 'Don't know what they are yet. But the message was we gotta help 'em.'

He turned to Kix. 'Don't be so quick to judge, my little Imp. Lena is very good. And 'sides, what other choice do you have? Do *you* know how to heal your friend?'

Kix stared at him a long moment, before finally lowering her gaze.

'Just don't mess it up. He's . . . special.'

Lena whistled through her teeth. 'Well, I've never known any of you Axis types be so attached to your droids before.'

BitZer clambered to the top of Kix's scarf. 'Well you haz now.'

Lena frowned as she caught sight of his arm. 'That's a nasty burn you got, too.'

'Fix him first.' BitZer glanced around at the assorted plastics and wires lying on the table. 'I reckon I can DIY myself with what you got lying here.'

Lena nodded, and examined Michio's face closely. Then she sighed. 'It doesn't look good at all. I'm going to have to put him under.'

Kix caught her breath.

'A full shut down? But you don't have his revival software.'

'I know, but he's got to be cold metal for me to get as deep as I need.'

'Don't talk about him like he's just a machine.'

Lena raised an eyebrow. 'You're lucky you've found me. Around here people'd melt him as fast as look at him.'

'Heathens,' muttered Kix. And then, bending low over Michio, she whispered in his ear, 'Don't you dare die on me, you hear?'

And then to her amazement, his eyes fluttered open.

'Flower, Bird, Wind, Moon,' he whispered.

Kix gasped. 'You're alive!'

His gentle eyes met hers. 'The hope is bigger than me. If I do not live it passes onto you.'

Her eyes flashed. 'You can't lay that on me.'

Michio smiled faintly. 'You must . . . find GERILLR, he is the . . . key. People . . . deserve . . . the truth.' He turned his head slowly to Lena. 'Please, proceed.'

She nodded. 'I will do the best I can.'

'After the earth, the rain hardens,' he sighed, his eyes falling shut again.

'What does that mean?' asked Lena.

BitZer sighed. 'Dang our donglez if any of uz knowz. Just fix him, lady. *Pleaze*.'

Unbuttoning Michio's tunic, Lena uncovered a flat panel on his chest. Opening it, she picked up a long fine needle and inserted it into a hole in the centre of the panel, before injecting a clear fluid into the cavity. A few seconds later, Michio's limbs fell limp and his head lolled to the side.

BitZer puffed out his cheeks. 'Oh, I feelz lower than a snake in snowshoez.'

Lena glanced at him. 'Leave me now. All of you. I need to concentrate.'

19

Snorri beckoned Kix and BitZer to join him and the other pirates who were now gathered in an excited circle at the far end of the bunker.

'Come on, girl. Nows it's our turn to ask the questions. Who are yer and how did yer get here?'

Kix shook her head as she crossed the room.

'We're just a bunch of Shade City outkasts. And as for how we got here . . . we don't know. Not really.'

'You don't know how you just outran DEVA?' Snorri glanced around at the others. 'We could do with some of that *don't know* ourselves.'

They chuckled.

'It isn't funny,' growled Kix.

'No. A thing of wonder is what it is.' Snorri's eyes flashed with excitement. 'Strange things are afoot. All we know is we was hit with a mad energy surge and then a message dropped from out of nowhere tellin' us to rescue you.

What do yer know about that?'

Kix sighed. 'Something. But it's nuts.'

Snorri spread his arms. 'Try us.'

Kix took a deep breath. 'The energy surge that hit you is a wormhole that a crazy scientist cooked up, to join two worlds – Deva and another planet called Earth – together in parallel universes.'

Snorri started to laugh. 'That's im—'

'Impossible. I know. And also true.'

'How you think we gotz all the way from Texida to here in less than a second? Rip carried uz,' muttered BitZer from the table, waving a fistful of wires at the group.

Snorri shook his head. 'Even if it's true, what's it to do with us pirates? Yer said you were told to look for us . . .'

Kix shrugged. 'Don't know again.'

He narrowed his eyes. 'What exactly is your beef with DEVA?'

'It's not just DEVA. It's *Önska*.'

A murmur broke out amongst the group.

'The Kat herself is after you?'

'Yes. She found out about the wormhole . . .' Kix swallowed. 'And she wants to use it to dump a deadly fuel algae onto Earth. That's why she's grabbed Mikey. If she has him, she controls the rip, you see.'

Snorri rubbed his forehead. 'Wait now. Mikey? Who's that?'

'A – kind of boy from Earth.'

'A kind of boy? What's he doing here, if he's from Earth? And why will the Kat control the rip if she has him? This is madness.'

Kix curled her lip. 'Welcome to our world.'

'Allz you need to know,' cut in BitZer, 'iz Mikey got dragged here through the wormhole and it'z a terrible mistake, but the thing can't be shut until we sendz him back. And all you needz to know about Önska iz she'z gone koko loko. If she dumpz the UltraRed in the wormhole the chancez are it'll destroy either uz or the other planet. Or both, if you'z feeling apokolypso.'

A slender girl in skinny, fur-trimmed jeans stepped forward.

'The UltraRed? We've heard rumours about that. They say it's eating the ocean alive.'

Kix nodded. 'It is. Imagine if it got in the wormhole.'

The girl shook her head. 'And the only way to prevent that is to close the rip. Is that what you're saying?'

'Yes.'

'So what's stopping you?'

Kix snorted. 'What isn't? One, we don't know how to shut it. Two, we don't know where the mouth of the rip is.

207

Three, like I said, we need Mikey. Four, we're up against the Kat.'

Silence fell on the group. Snorri turned to Kix.

'This is a mighty pickle. Is this everything yer know?'

'Well, the only thing I've left out is there's this person we're trying to find. Michio thinks he's the answer to everything . . .'

'Who?'

Kix flushed. 'We don't rightly know. All we know for sure is he's a digital freedom fighter who was spying on Xenon Deva on Earth when his experiment blew up. He's a bit like you guys, I suppose.'

'And why do you need him?'

'Because he brought all of us together when he appeared on Deva.'

'But you don't know where he is now?'

'Nope. Our best guess is he's hiding in the digisphere in the Reef somewhere.'

'When did all this happen?'

Kix chewed her lip. 'Two days ago.'

'The time?'

'8:17 p.m. I know exactly because that's when my Koral quit on me.'

Uproar broke out amongst the group.

'But that's exactly when we got the virus!' cried the girl.

Kix looked at her. 'What virus?'

'The one to crash DEVA.'

'Do you know who sent it?'

'No name. Only a golden ape, stamped at the end of its DNA—'

'Hella howdee doo deez! Finally, a bit of luck!' BitZer threw down the piece of plastic he was melting and leaped to his feet.

Kix stared, wide-eyed. 'That's him!'

'Who?'

'GERILLR. Who we're looking for – the golden ape is his icon. But how did he contact you?'

Snorri nodded to the girl.

'Snake, come to the middle so everyone can hear ye.'

Flushing a deep red, the slender girl stepped into the centre of the circle.

'I can't tell you how he found us – the file flew up from the deep digisphere. We didn't know what the message was at first – and when we opened it up we nearly died. The virus your guy has created is a killer. It's called Zoox, modelled on the symbiotic algae that keep coral reefs alive in the ocean. Corals are completely dependent on these dudes, wouldn't be able to survive without them since they can't make enough food themselves.'

'Yeah, but that's in the ocean. How does it work for real?' asked Kix impatiently.

'Same way, but digitally. If we aim it at DEVA'S central communication core, it'll reach a tipping point and bloom.'

'What will that do?'

'Bleach out DEVA's entire communications network, including the Reef.'

'For how long?'

'Not sure till we try. Could only be a few seconds, but that might be enough for us to find this GERILLR guy if he's out there.'

Kix shook her head. 'Won't their defencebots just wipe out the Zoox on sight?'

Snake shrugged. 'Maybe. Maybe not. As I say, the virus is real smart; it's got all these weird, organic algorhythms that the bots will probably never have seen before. Makes sense if they were created on another planet.' She paused. 'But if this wormhole is as dangerous as you say it is, we can't just let the Kat get away with it. We got to go on the offensive.'

There was silence for a moment. Then Kix began to laugh.

'No offence guys, but be real. This is DEVA we're talking about.'

Snorri cocked his head to the side. 'Do you know why

we pick the lock every time we enter the cave?'

'No,' she sighed. 'But I guess you're about to tell me.'

'Because when you pick a lock you understand that all barriers in your environment, all limits, are in your head. An' that you hold the key.'

BitZer whistled. 'Oh, boyz. An we thought Michio waz bad.'

Snorri gave a bark of laughter. 'Listen. We're not stupid dreamers. Most of us here are ex-Kalasia Axis engineers. We had good jobs, good lives, but we *defected.* '

'You left?' Kix's eyes widened in shock.

A smile hovered over his lips. 'Yeah. Why? You never thought to get out?'

'And do what? There's nothing else.'

'That's your fear talking. That's what DEVA is banking on. They want everyone to believe they're invincible. Total Information Awareness, right? And so they suck down every piece of data they can find on you. Yer history, browsing, biometrics, medical records, credit-card transactions, upgrades – you name it, they got it. And that's how they control you.'

'We know,' said Kix. 'We're Imperfectibles.'

'But they're not as powerful as they want you to believe. They're relying on *you* to make them bigger than they are.'

'They still got a whole lot of control.'

211

'Aye, they do. But being big has become their Achilles heel. It means when faced with an attack, they've got a whole lot of defendin' to do, whereas little old us, all we've got to do is find one weakness and we're in.'

Snake nodded. 'It's so long since anyone attacked DEVA. It might take them by surprise.'

Kix shook her head. 'But I don't understand why you'd do this. This isn't your problem.'

Snorri crossed his powerful arms. 'It is if we make it our problem. And 'sides. It sounds like fun, right?' He glanced around the group, his blue eyes alight. 'If we do this, there'll be no coming back, amigos. Once the Korporation work out who crashed them they'll be after our skins. So we've got to pray that GERILLR, whoever he is, is waiting for us on the other side. Waddya reckon?'

The pirates looked around at each other, their faces pale in the flickering, indigo light.

Their breath came white on the freezing air. 'Hell, yes!' they cried.

'Then let's get to work. Let loose the Zoox!'

The group dissolved instantly as the pirates flew to their task. Kix turned to look at Lena. She was still bent low over Michio's open chest at the far end of the table.

BitZer snuggled up to her ear.

'He'z gotta make it, Kix. We owez him,' he whispered.

She nodded. 'I know. And I mean to pay the debt – as long as we can stay alive ourselves.'

He waved a cable in the air, setting off a trail of sparks. 'But . . . if we don't survive, at least we'll haz checked out with style.'

'Thought you told me to keep well out of Buddhabot freedom nonsense. *We can't fix what can't be fixed*, you said.'

'I knowz I did . . .' BitZer looked around the bunker, at the pirates furiously preparing the Zoox at their monitors. 'But theze peepz . . . they'z got me all sentimental. Look at em, in their raggedy fur and all . . . They got ballz, Kixie. They'z taking on the Korporation . . . doing what we'z been too chicken to do.'

'Hey, BitZerbot, I reckon that acid burned out more than your arm. You're talking like a Badlander. Don't forget the only reason we've kept ourselves alive all this time is by keeping our heads down.'

He looked up at her, his cobalt eyes gleaming.

'I knowz. But maybe I don't just want to survive no more . . . maybe I wantz to live.'

Kix whistled. 'Maybe you want too much, little brother.'

He jammed his hands on his little hips. 'Ah, theze piratez haz gotten under your skin too, girl pie, and don't you dare deny it.'

'I don't think so—!'

She was interrupted by a sharp tap on her arm.

'Here.'

Kix whirled round to see Snorri holding out a rough beach pebble.

'What's that?'

'Pirate ID. For you. We need all the hackers we can get.'

She frowned. 'I'm not using that. DEVA hates you even more than me. They'd double kill me.'

Snorri grinned. 'Aye, out of the frying pan into the fire. But at least you'd be back in the game again.' He dropped the pebble onto the table in front of her and walked away, whistling.

Kix stared down at it for a long time. And then, slowly, she reached out and picked it up. And as her fingers tightened around its cool surface, she felt the familiar tingle of *connection*. She turned and gave BitZer a wry look.

'Gotta be in it . . .'

'To win it!' he hissed, his tiny shoulders trembling with laughter. 'You an Imp *and* a Pirate now. You'z way too hotz to handle, girl!'

20

Nero glanced up at his screen before bending over the ship's communicator.

'Move into formation,' he ordered, smiling grimly as he watched the fleet of massive helitankers begin to descend on a patch of frothing, crimson UltraRed lying off the Gulf of Texida. Skimming the water's surface at 105 knots, each flying tanker was capable of sucking up ten million litres in seconds. Nero's smile broadened. Ah, how he loved his machine family. So elegant. So dependable. So very, very happy to do as they were told.

Nonetheless, he cast an anxious glance at the time. According to his calculations, once the helitankers had sucked up the UltraRed, it would only take the algae a few hours to eat its way out of the giant tanks. He sighed. The only way of pulling off this crazy stunt was to find the mouth of the wormhole in super-fast time so they could dump the UltraRed in. The Kat had not told him how she was planning to do that . . . And even if they did succeed in finding the mouth, who knew what would happen once they started pouring millions of tons of sex-crazed nanosludge into it . . . With every hour, the rip was growing more unpredictable and powerful. He'd just had a report that all of Deva's swans had turned black overnight.

Nero swallowed. His loyalty programming was being stretched to breaking point. The. Whole. Thing. Was. Insane. But how could he contravene a direct order from the boss? On the other hand, countered his logic circuits, if the order was given by an unhappy fat Burmese algorithm, did he still have to follow it? Yes, replied a different bunch of circuits, reminding him that his sole purpose was to serve the Korporation. Nero's shoulders drooped. He wasn't made for thinking outside the box.

And then a thought flared up from a bunch of rogue neurons on the very edge of the edge of his box. Nero sucked in a nonexistent breath . . . he was dangerously close to having an original thought . . . What if *he* didn't have to be disloyal? What if he merely assisted someone *else* in taking the Kat out? That wouldn't be so bad, would it? A thrill ran through him as the outline of a plan began to take shape. It was risky, for if Önska discovered what he was up to, she'd melt him down on the spot. Nero squared his shoulders. He'd have to be careful. Oh so very careful.

He was suddenly yanked out of his plotting by an alarm siren coming from the screen. Twisting his neck, he stared at the helitankers and frowned. Something was terribly wrong. For, instead of soaring in a perfect V over the red ocean, the tankers were now flying in weird circles over the sea like drugged dragonflies.

He grabbed the intercom. 'Group Leader? What is your status?'

His screen now filled with a horribly pixellated feed of the cockpit of the lead helitanker. He could just make out a SPIDR pilot, desperately pulling back on the manual controls with all eight legs.

'Talk to me!' bellowed Nero.

'No control . . . instruments – dead!' hissed the SPIDR. And then, to Nero's horrified eyes, the helitanker engine sputtered and cut out.

'Mayday, mayday!' came the SPIDR's final desperate cry before the ship plummeted into a nosedive and crashed into the red sea – followed by all the others. In seconds, the entire fleet had disappeared underwater.

'No! No!' gasped Nero, but before he could react, the

bridge beneath him tilted as the ship slid onto its side with a great groan of collapsing metal. Grabbing onto the control panel, Nero pulled the alarm lever. But it was no use. Every single winking, twinkling, blinking light in the panel had faded, every instrument was dead. He thumped the desk in fury. What now?

* * *

Across the Reef, the Zoox Virus was multiplying at ferocious speed. It was one nasty piece of work. Imagine the Great Plague multiplied by the most suppurating buboes ever to fester in a man's armpit, add in one hundred and forty-four thousand frothing Norwegian rats and subtract one final pitiful cry of a starving puppy and you will have some idea of its horror and power. From the moment it breached the first of the DEVA defences, it was unstoppable.

And as it moved into the centre of DEVA's network, it immediately copied itself at each node before going on to attack the next connection. Doubling, quadrupling, octupling and whatever the next term is every nanosecond, the virus not only spread, but it learned as it went along, swarming up the Korporation's privilege levels like a rat up a drainpipe. The defencebots had never seen anything like it. With each passing moment, the Zoox became exponentially more and more intelligent until finally, with a brilliant burst of colour, it *bloomed* and the impossible possibled.

DEVA *crashed*.

And two things happened instantly:

1) 9,000,000,000,000,000,000,000,000,000,000,000,000,000,000,000 billion credits were wiped off the Korporation's share price, but within .58 of a second the losses were rolled up as debt, repackaged and sold off as horsemeat stocks. All of this was done without any fuss or fanfare by a small dusty computer sitting quietly in a locked filing cabinet in Penge, South London. Nobody knows why, although it has subsequently come to light that on Önska's pedigree papers her place of birth is listed as the Kokney Kitty Kattery in Katford, South London. You can make your own mind up as to whether this is a coincidence or not.

2) On the Reef, every single file – every message, every mail, every tweet, every military secret, every password, every bank account number, everything anyone was sure (double sure) they'd deleted – resurfaced, opened and lay there, quivering in the harsh digital glare for all to read. The Reef was open. Privacy was dead. DEVA was down and the Zoox had done its work.

* * *

In the ice bunker, the pirates stared, dumbfounded, at the

carnage unfolding on their screens.

'It worked!' breathed Kix into the silence.

Snorri threw his head back and gave a great belly laugh.

'I never thought I'd live to see such a thing. DEVA, flat on its back.'

'It'll only have worked if we find GERILLR,' hissed Snake. 'Let's get out on the Reef before the counter-attack comes.'

Snorri nodded. Holding high his ID pebble, he stared around at the pirates. Each of them was poised in front of a device or screen.

'Find him, me hearties!' he shouted, his voice echoing in the icy chamber. 'And turn the Korporation upside down if yer have to.'

And with that he dropped into the Reef. Kix stared for a few seconds. And then, snatching up her pebble, she jumped in behind him.

* * *

Mikey struggled to right himself in his cell. The ship had keeled over to one side and he was upside down, pressed against the bars. He could hear angry shouting coming from somewhere and he peered out into the gloom of the passageway outside, desperate to know what was going on.

'Hey!' he shouted. 'What's going on?'

But his voice bounced off the corridor walls and died away. No one was interested. The needs of one little prisoner were small fry compared to the unthinkable thing that was happening to the Korporation.

On the bridge, Nero finally succeeded in pulling himself upright.

Önska clawed her way across the walls to his side.

'Nero! Whut is goin on?' she demanded, hooking herself onto the sinews of his thigh.

He swept his gaze over the dead instruments. 'DEVA has crashed.'

'What do you mean *crashed*?' she hissed. 'We don't crash. *Ever.*'

'Well we just have. But ma'am, be assured, the defencebots will be massing.'

'To Hel with them. What r u doing?' she yowled.

'This.'

Bending over the console, Nero stuck his fingers inside a dead light gauge and, yanking out a chip, he scanned it. On his screen, a tiny organism appeared, burrowing deep in the chip's innards. 'There you are . . .' growled Nero. 'I am going to start a counterattack right now. I have a feeling I know what caused this.'

Önska stared at the wriggly thing.

'Whuts that?'

'If I'm not mistaken, it's the virus that has just crashed us.'

'Are dose Imps behind this?'

Nero held it up to his eye as he ran a scan.

'It was launched from Iceland, ma'am. But its components are strange . . . non Devan.'

The Kat chittered in rage. 'O, its dem allright. They must hav joind up wiv the pirates. Everybody knoes that Reykjavik is a vipr's nest ov 'em. When we're back up, I'm gonna oblitrate teh whole dirty, freezy place.' She extended her claws to their full length. Not since the Great Kat Koup had she been so furious.

Activating his illuminator, Nero shone a brilliant beam on the magnified Zoox. Taking out a scalpel, he sliced its body open and inspected its entrails. He bit back a gasp when he saw how high up the DEVA hierarchy it had penetrated. It had to be stopped *now*.

Shutting off all ancillary body parts, the android directed all of his processing power to his brain. He sat, perfectly motionless, as he examined the Zoox, running loop after loop of possible counter-attack options. The thing seemed so basic . . . how had it pierced their defences? And then he smiled as the truth dawned on him. The virus had worked because the defencebots simply didn't recognise it. *Because it was from Earth.* But beyond that it was pitifully simple – each time it attacked a new node, the first thing it did was check that another copy of itself wasn't living there. If it was, the virus simply deleted itself. All he had to do was engineer a fake Zoox and inject it across the Reef. The original creation would destroy itself in minutes.

His fingers a blur, he cut the Zoox into fragments and reassembled its code until he'd engineered a perfect copy. Then he reinserted the fake Zoox back into the light-gauge chip and slotted it back into the instrument panel.

'Take that!' he muttered. Seconds passed, then a few more and then, to his joy, lights began to flicker back to life on his instrument panel. He'd started the fight back. The virus was already beginning to die on the ship. In a few moments he'd have his communicator back and then he could contact DEVA's central core – and from there it would take no time at all for his antidote to free the Reef.

He turned to Önska.

'Mission accomplished, ma'am. The virus will soon be dead.'

She glanced at him. 'Nice work, machine.'

'Thank you.' Nero inclined his head respectfully,

but inside he was cold, metallic fury. The Zoox had made a fool out of DEVA, out of the defencebots – his people. When this attack was repelled, he would personally go after the perpetrators and flame them into hot ash.

* * *

On the Reef, Kix whirled round as a bank of lights to her left began to flicker and spark. The place was coming back to life – the defencebots must be starting to push the Zoox back. Surfacing for a second, Kix glanced around the bunker. All the pirates were deep inside but nobody seemed to be getting anywhere. Not even Snorri. Time was running out.

BitZer shook his little head. 'Thiz iz hopeless. Why don't we go look for GERILLR in the data tunnel . . . y'know, the place we first saw himz?'

She frowned. 'How? Nobody could survive that deep in the digisphere – for real or plugged in.'

'You gotz any better ideaz?'

She shrugged. 'Nope.'

'Then let's go, Kaloux.'

'OK, then.'

Diving back into the virtual world, Kix turned from the main Reef highway and ducked into the weed-choked dirty code that lined the edges of the software. After searching for a few seconds, she found what she was looking for, a half-buried access point. Checking the code, she saw it was wide enough to get her down there – *just*.

She glanced at BitZer.

'You up for this?'

'Yez'm.'

'Then hold tight.'

Grabbing onto the porthole, she leaped into the tunnel. Data streamed past them at terrifying velocity as they plunged downwards.

Kix stared, wide eyed. 'BitZ, we've got to stop and pick up a few bits. This stuff is worth a fortune.'

'Quit itz!' he hissed.

A moment later, they landed on the corroded metal of the tunnel floor. Picking herself up, Kix jerked her thumb to the left. 'This way . . . We're pretty close to that big junction where we met Mikey, I reckon.'

BitZer cupped his hands around his mouth.

'Oi, GERILLR!'

His voice bounced brittle off the tunnel walls, but there was no reply. Kix set off towards the junction, BitZer calling out GERILLR's name every few seconds until they rounded the final bend and reached the place where they'd first seen him.

'This is it, right?' whispered Kix. 'It looks so different from inside the Reef.'

BitZer nodded. 'Thiz is it all rightz. GERILLR! Holler if you can hear uz.'

But his cry was only met with more silence.

Kix sighed. 'It's no good, BitZ. He's not here.' She whirled around as the tunnel generators hummed into life. 'Listen! The Reef safety systems are reviving. We need to get gone.'

Turning on her heel, she began to retrace her footsteps, but before she'd taken a couple of paces, the tip of her cowboy boot hit something, sending it skittering across the tunnel floor.

'Whatz that?' asked BitZer.

'Dunno.' Accessing her night vision, Kix bent down and began to search the floor. After a few moments her eye fell on a small, tarnished disk lying against the wall.

'Hey, look – it's my burnt-out memory file from the other day.'

BitZer jumped to the ground. 'Hellz bellz!' he cried, before poking at it with a bendy forefinger. But the moment he touched the file, he flew backwards, hitting the wall hard.

'You all right?' asked Kix, rushing over to his side.

He lay dazed.

'BitZ?'

Slowly, his eyes came back into focus.

'Iza Kane.'

'What?'

'Iza. Kane. That's your sister's name.'

Kix grabbed him. 'What are you talking about?'

'When I just touched the hologram disk, the name flew into me . . .' BitZer trailed off.

'But Iza Kane is that reality star, the one with the hit show on *360 People* . . .'

'I knowz.'

'So she can't be my sister . . .'

Bitzer shrugged. 'Dunno Kix. That's the name I got. The Zoox must've opened up the data in there . . . an I gotz it like a barrel tween both eyez.'

'Are you sure?'

He shook his head. 'I izn't sure bout nothing.'

'Anything else?'

'Nope.' BitZer got gingerly to his feet. 'An' you won't find no morez. That file he burnt good.' He burst into amazed laughter. 'In-cre-di-blez! After all our searching we got a clue.'

'I can't believe it,' gasped Kix.

He put his hand out. 'We'll hunt her down, I promise. But laterz. We gotta do thiz job first.'

Kix sighed. 'Well we're flopping it big time. GERILLR's not here.'

'So we go look somewherez else.'

She suddenly jerked her head upwards, peering behind him at the tunnel wall.

'What's that?'

'Whatz?'

She took a step towards the corroded wall. In the dark, she could just make out some rough symbols painted on its uneven surface.

'Those weren't here before, were they?'

'Don't reckon they waz.' BitZer's eyes glittered as he turned. 'Get some light going for me, willya?'

Kix fumbled to access her light beam again. Activating it, she turned back to the wall to see two lines of symbols scrawled across it.

46° 14' 03" N

6° 03' 10" E

'What's that?'

'Looks like lat and longitude coordinatez for somewherez.'

'Where?'

BitZer tapped his tiny teeth. 'Beatz me.'

'Look. There's something else, just underneath the lower line,' said Kix, bending down. They both drew closer. And there, set a few centimetres beneath the numbers was a tiny, rough image of a golden ape.

'Got him!' screamed BitZer.

Kix covered her mouth in amazement.

'It's him!'

BitZer turned again to look at the lines of numbers.

'He must be trying to send uz there.'

'Where?'

'The mouth of the rip maybe?'

Kix clenched her fist.

'Let's get back and tell the others.'

'Yez, ma'am!'

'You got the coordinates stored?'

He tapped his head.

'Burnt in!'

Giving one last look around the tunnel, Kix tapped her pirate ID pebble. Immediately the Reef dissolved behind her and she was once again sitting at the long table in the ice bunker.

'Pull out, everyone. I found him!' she cried.

Snorri turned towards her, his eyes blazing with excitement.

'All right, yer heard the lady,' he cried, banging on the table. 'Everybody out!'

In a matter of seconds, the pirates reemerged from

the Reef – and not a moment too soon. Snake was the last to exit – and as she pulled herself free, a great blaze of energy ripped through the dead space, reanimating it with digital life.

The Zoox had been destroyed.

DEVA was back in control.

21

The pirates gathered around Kix and BitZer as they told them about what they'd discovered.

Snorri's eyes widened. 'Well, what are we waiting for? Let's load the co-ordinates up.'

Snake wagged her finger. 'No. Wait. If we search on the reef then DEVA will know them too.' She turned to a pirate to her left. 'Haven't we got an old world map?'

He shrugged. 'Well, yeah, but it might fall to pieces soon as we open it.'

'Go get it.'

In a moment he was back. Unfolding the map, Snake gingerly smoothed the yellowing squares out over the table. They watched breathlessly as she located the numbers until, finally, her finger came to rest on the intersection point. She frowned.

'Swizzleland? That can't be right,' she muttered.

'Do it again,' muttered Snorri.

231

Snake swiftly recalculated but came up with precisely the same result.

There was a moment's silence as they all stared at the spot on the map.

Kix scratched her head. 'But there's nothing there. I did a job in Swizzleland once. Nothing but two-thousand-year-old bankers and hot cheese.'

'Together? That's cool.'

'No it isn't.'

'Well, there *must* be something, otherwise why would GERILLR be directing us there?'

'Can't we find out more using a pirate ID? If anyone knows how to sneak around the Korporation, it's you.'

Snorri shook his head. 'Not this time. We've blown our cover sky-high with the Zoox attack. GERILLR must've given us these coordinates for a reason. If we can't go online, the only thing left to us is to get our arses over there to find out why.'

Kix sucked her teeth. 'Us?'

He laid his hand on her arm. 'Well, you, actually.'

'Excuse me?'

Snorri grinned. 'I've got a job to do – and all the other pirates are needed for the defence, 'cos I'll bet my bottom dollar there's a fleet of Predators coming this way. The only ones we can spare are you and the BitZerbot.'

She stared around wildly. 'Oh yeah? And just what job is that?'

'Me and Snake has just cooked up a plan. We're going to spring Mikey. No point you finding the mouth of the rip if we don't have him to throw in, right?'

Kix cocked her head. 'And how are you gonna find him?'

Snorri clapped Snake on the shoulder. 'Tell her.'

The girl turned. 'I managed to capture one piece of data while I was in the core.'

'Whatz?' asked BitZer curiously.

Snake tapped her ID pebble. 'The root key for DEVA's I Am So Special program.'

BitZer's eyes lit up. 'That's their deluxe package izn't it? What you planning to do with it, Snakez?'

'Rustle up a little mayhem. Root gives me total control over a whole bunch of their most wealthy customers.'

BitZer whistled. 'Oh my. You gonna have yusselvez a par-tay!'

'That's the plan. In no time, DEVA will be begging me to stop.'

'And will you?'

Snake nodded. 'Oh yes. But the price will be Mikey.'

'The Fat Kat will never give him up.'

'Then she'll have to decide what's more dangerous.

Fifty thousand out o' control High Net Worthers or the UltraRed.'

Kix grinned. 'Snake. That is evil.'

Snake grinned back. 'I know.'

Snorri jerked his thumb at the bunker radar screen. 'Won't be long before they're here. You gotta go now while there's still time.'

A voice came from the far side of the table.

'Guys, it is time to wake him!'

They turned. Lena had straightened from Michio's side and was now beckoning them over.

'I have done what I can,' she said softly.

Stepping over to the table, Kix watched as Lena gently pressed the needle back into Michio's chest. BitZer crept onto her shoulder and together they stared down at his scarred face.

Kix squeezed her palms together. 'Come on,' she whispered. Michio's face was peaceful, but it looked old – old and yet beautiful, as if all the gentleness in his nature had remoulded the plastics in its image.

Lena withdrew the needle. 'It might take a few minutes.'

But a few minutes passed, and Michio didn't move. And nor did he move the next minute, nor the one after that.

Kix bit back tears. How could she leave him now?

* * *

Captain Duchamp II leaned against the shattered window of his grounded Quadrocopter and stared tragically over the frozen Icelandic sea ice. He'd so nearly pulled it off – he'd located Kix and BitZer on the beach, but when he'd flown in to capture them a few minutes later, they'd vanished. Where to, he couldn't imagine – the place was a barren wasteland – but he'd kept his cool and begun to sweep the area inch by frozen inch. And then suddenly his ship had fallen out of the sky. Like a stone.

Duchamp breathed out carefully between his teeth. He had no idea why he'd crash-landed at this godforsaken spot and after the day he'd had, he didn't care. He was feeling emotional. He was feeling unloved. He was feeling *dangereuse*.

He raised a weary eyebrow at the deskSPIDR who had scuttled onto the monitor deck.

'What?'

It rubbed its forefeet together excitedly. 'Good news, sir. Our Quadrocopter will soon be operational again. Our crash was caused by a viral attack on DEVA's core, but it has been repelled.' And then, when the Captain didn't reply, the SPIDR rubbed its legs a little more. 'That's good isn't it, sir? We can proceed with the attack.

According to the scanner, the pirates are occupying a space behind the ice wall.'

Duchamp shook his head grimly. 'And then what? We kill them all, I suppose?'

'Er . . . Yes sir.'

'And will that make you feel good, eh, SPIDR?'

The poor creature took an unhappy sideways step. It simply didn't have the energy for the Captain's existential crisis. It made a note to itself to only work under stupid officers after this. But as it shrank back against the control panel, the Quadrocopter thruster engines suddenly hummed back into life and the lights flooded back on, dazzling the Captain. But when he was able to see again, it was to view Önska's enormous face on the bridge screen. Duchamp groaned inside. Was there no escaping the Kitten of Death?

She fixed him with a cold eye.

'Duchamp. Where r u?'

He offered up a jerky salute.

'Iceland, madam. I was forced into an emergencie landing.'

'Have u located teh hostiles?'

He nodded. 'Bien sûr. According to my instruments, they are right over la, behind the cliff.'

A repulsive smile rippled around her overbite. 'U r sure?' she hissed.

'Oui. You told me to follow them and I did. What are your orders?'

'The same. Destroy dem. Immediatly.'

His face dropped. 'But I don't know how many they are. They are maybe a large crew of pirates also. I need back-up.'

The air screen filled with a close-up of Önska's claw hovering over Duchamp's I Am package.

'Don't make me do it, Captain.'

Duchamp stood a moment, clenching and unclenching his fist.

'Fine,' he muttered. 'I – I will go in alone and destroy them as you ask.'

She cocked her chubby head. 'Hardly lone, Captain. U still hav teh tank and all teh weapons in ur Quadrocoptr. And these peeps r only Imps and Badlanders in teh end. Do dis, and u will be rewardd well.'

The screen went blank.

Duchamp turned to his scanner. The ice was blocking the accuracy of his heat sensors, making it impossible to count the pirate numbers. He made a mental review of the weapon options available to him. And then his lip curled. Sound. He'd make those little devils dance by blasting them with a Super Loud Sound Barrage. Accessing the track options, he glanced down the list before selecting a song. Extending his finger, he punched the play button and immediately a two-hundred decibel barrage of *Je Ne Regret Rien* blasted out at the ice wall.

* * *

Inside the bunker, madness broke out. The pirates threw themselves to the ground, covering their ears against the terrible noise. Snorri crawled over to Kix.

'Predators!' he bellowed. 'They must've have flown under our radar. We've got to get out of here.'

Kix ignored him. Bending over Michio, she cupped his head in her hands.

'Wake up!' she cried.

But the synthetic remained completely motionless, his face like a death mask.

Snorri pulled at her arm urgently. 'Now!' he screamed.

Kix started to drag Michio off the table. 'I'm taking him with us!'

Snorri grabbed both her shoulders. 'He's gone, Kix.'

'He'z right,' sobbed BitZer from her scarf.

Her eyes flashed as she yelled, 'What would have happened if I'd abandoned *you* all those years ago?'

'I knowz, but we've got a planet to save, girl,' BitZer screamed, flinging his arms in the air in despair.

Kix gave a deep, trembling sigh, holding Michio for a

long moment against her chest before laying him down on the table again. How could she leave behind someone who'd sacrificed himself to save BitZer – the only family she had. But she knew she had to. With eyes half-blind with tears, she followed the others as they began to stumble down the secret exit.

Behind her, Snorri was the last to leave the bunker. As he stepped into the passageway, he turned for one last look at the little figure lying amongst the wires and cables. Snorri balled his fists. It went against every sinew in his pirate body to leave a comrade behind.

'Hold on, I'm comin' back!' he cried, starting to retrace his steps, but before he'd taken even four paces, a shell exploded above him and he was hurled to the ground. A deep crack appeared in the bunker walls. Cursing the Predators, Snorri dragged himself to his knees and crawled back down the escape passage. He was no good to anyone dead.

After he'd gone, the bunker lay eerily still in the aftermath of the explosion. The only movement was the waves of pulsing light that still played across its icy walls from the screens. And then, slowly, slowly, Michio opened one eye. With a great effort, he raised himself onto his elbow and brought his right hand up to his face. Gasping with strain, he activated his palm-screen camera and set it to record. A red flashing light appeared on screen. Swallowing hard, Michio began to speak.

* * *

At the mouth of the exit tunnel, the pirates crouched, waiting for Snorri.

'As soon as he gets here we split,' whispered Snake.

'Are you really going to go after Önska?' asked Kix.

Snake grinned. 'Hell, yeah!'

'You sure?'

'Yes.' Snake glanced anxiously down the passage behind them. 'Where is he?'

'Here,' came the pirate's whispered reply as he finally emerged from the tunnel. He grasped Kix by the hand. 'Now you do your thing and we'll do ours – and we'll see yer up high in the Swizzleland.' He rubbed his nose, violently. 'And for what it's worth, you two are all right. I never knew Kalasia people could be so . . . well, like us.'

Kix gave him a wry look. 'Not sure how to take that, dude.'

He gave her a sly look back. 'As a compliment, Lady Kix.'

Snake tutted. 'Hey guys, enough lovin'.' She pointed to the left. 'Follow this path along the beach. It'll bring you out above the port. There, take the trail for a few minutes and you'll come to a fir wood where there's a flying car hidden under the branches. Drive under the contours till you're well over the ocean.'

Behind them there was another dull thud of an explosion. Kix turned to look back down the passageway.

'I can't believe we're leaving him.'

Snake sighed. 'No choice. Farewell.'

And with that, she leaped onto the frozen shingle, the pirates following behind. Within seconds they were lost in the dark shadows of the winter beach.

Kix reached up to tuck BitZer into the folds of her scarf. 'Well come on then, buddy. And hold tight. You'll freeze your little bollox off if you fall overboard.'

'Overboard? Iz that like a pirate term, Kixie?' he giggled.

'Just hold on tight and shut up.'

And with that she set off along the icy path towards the port.

* * *

Emerging from the Quadrocopter, the armoured tank paused on the beach. Captain Duchamp lowered the gun barrel, firing a long, lethal blaze of light at the ice wall, which immediately collapsed in a great, frozen slide. He then nosed the tank forward over the shattered cliff.

Duchamp smiled as he caught a miniscule flicker of

life on his thermal imager. *Ah, there they were.* Idiots. Did they really think a bit of ice could protect them from him? He drove the tank forward, the flickering glow growing stronger and stronger as he progressed. He sighed. It was pathetically easy, really. No fun at all. He tightened his hands upon the wheel, pushing down his emotions. No time for sentimentality. His job was to get in, wipe them out and leave. Then he and his old maman could live another day.

In a few moments, he reached the bunker wall and, revving up the tank engine, he smashed through the doorway and swung the gun barrel into position. Then he flipped on the intercom.

'Hello, mes amis. I know you are here. Surrender or die. You have ten seconds.'

Duchamp watched dispassionately as the numbers on the countdown clock quietly clicked down from ten. As the counter neared the zero, he tightened his finger around the trigger. And then, just as he was about to rake the room with a barrage of bullets, he suddenly became aware that a small figure was standing directly in front of the tank. He immediately extended a gripper arm, yanking the figure up into the bright arc of the tank searchlight.

Duchamp gasped as he caught sight of its face. 'Oh? So

we meet again, Professor Mori. You cheated death once, but this time I think *non*.'

Michio turned his exhausted face to the light. 'Neither of us are going to cheat death, my friend.'

The Captain raised a scornful Gallic eyebrow. 'Ho! I ne pas think so. I am Duchamp II, first class Predator officer . . .'

Michio smiled. 'Yes. But as soon as you make another error, you'll be a first-class tin can. It surprises me that you are still here. I know how the Kat operates.'

'Pah. You know nothing.'

Michio smiled gently. 'I can hear the fear in your voice. What did she threaten you with, my friend?'

'I am not your friend,' snapped Duchamp, but under the gentle gaze of Michio, he suddenly began to feel a little weepy. He couldn't help it, his chin began to tremble.

'Termination!' he whispered, trying to hold back tears he hadn't shed for twenty years.

'I don't mean to be . . . insensitive, but what else did you expect?'

Duchamp's shoulders started to shake. 'A little . . . loyalty.'

'From the Korporation?' Michio shook his head, his eyes now also gleaming with sympathetic tears. 'I repeat, we are more alike than you know.'

'Yes. They treat me like the chien. They treat you like the dog.'

Duchamp's shoulders now heaved with emotion and he burst into a wild outbreak of sobbing.

'It's good to let it all out,' murmured Michio, encouragingly.

Duchamp's head snapped up. 'Oui!' he cried with feeling. 'I am so mad my blood boils. And . . . you know I have no one to talk to. I am a Predator captain. It is a very macho business.'

Suppressing a gasp of pain, Michio forced himself to smile. 'But you are talking to me, now. Only we Korporation men can understand.'

Duchamp spat. 'Talking! What good will that do? Le Chat holds my life in her fat paws.'

'True. But there's still time to do something good.'

Duchamp frowned. 'What do you mean?'

'You could let us go.'

'Pah. Why would I do that?' muttered Duchamp.

'Because that way you'd be a hero, while still sticking it to the Kat.'

'How?'

'Because not only would you let us go, you'd tell her that you'd killed us. It would really mess with her plans. You know how much she wants us dead.'

For the first time all day, Duchamp's face lit up.

'That is true. But – it is so risky.'

'Not if you do it right.' Michio jerked his thumb over his shoulder. 'All you have to do is blast the hell out of the place. Might do you good. Release some tension, ha, ha. Why don't you blow up that wall right now? That'd make you feel better than twenty years of therapy.'

Duchamp's heart flamed up. It was tempting. Just for once, to let it all out. To be free. And before he knew what he was doing, he'd squeezed the trigger, releasing a searing blaze of energy that destroyed the rear wall of the bunker.

Michio grinned. 'That's better, eh? All those years of ass-kissing at the Academy. All those upgrade loans you'll never clear.'

Duchamp laughed wildly. 'Ooh, you are right! It feels so bon de bon!'

'Don't stop then!' cried Michio. 'Do the other wall. Pretend it's the Kitten you're aiming at!'

'Aaaiiiii!' screamed Duchamp, launching a rocket grenade in the direction of the secret passageway, collapsing the tunnel walls immediately.

Michio slapped his thigh. 'Amazing! No one could survive that. Now all you have to do is go back and tell the Kat we're dead.'

Duchamp set his lips. 'Oui. I will do this thing. I don't

understand what you have done to make her so angry. But whatever it is, I salute you, Korporation man.'

For a second they stared at each other along the long gun barrel and then, with a Gallic salute, Duchamp began to reverse the tank back out over the ice. His heart sang. Just that one act of rebellion had restored his pride – and as he headed back to the ship, he hit the play button and *Je Ne Regret Rien* began to echo over the frozen beach once more.

Behind him, Michio lay back down on the table, the last of his strength ebbing away from his body as silence fell once more on the shattered bunker. He just had to finish his recording and he was done.

22

Mikey gripped the bars of his cell. The ship was the right way up again, and the lights had come back on – but he was just as trapped as ever. His knuckles whitened around the bars. He had to get out of here. And then suddenly, he felt a vibration from inside his jacket. He patted himself down – and to his amazement, his fingers touched the rectangular outline of his tablet through the fabric – somehow the device had become trapped inside the lining. Mikey's mouth dropped open. How had that happened? With trembling fingers, he began to rip open the lining just as the tablet vibrated again. With a desperate tug at the fabric, he yanked it out. The screen immediately lit up with an incoming message. Mikey stared at it in shock.

> HEY MIKEY, IT'S GERILLA.

He couldn't move. Couldn't respond. The screen lit up again with another message.

> MIKEY NOT GOT LONG.

The boy forced his fingers down onto the keys.

> *Is that really you?*

He watched his cursor blinking in the message box, desperate for an answer to come.

> YEAH.

Mikey tightened his grip on the tablet.

> *Where are you?*

> DON'T KNOW 4 SURE.

> *Are you free?*

> NOT YET. ZOOK WS DESTROYD B4 I CUD BREAK FREE. BUT IT GAVE ME NUFF TIME 2 LEAK COORDIN8S 4 MOUTH OF WORMHLE.

Mikey shook his head.

> *What good is that if you and me aren't there?*

> HAVE FAITH. THE OTHERS R WORKING 2 GET U OUT. AND ILL B THERE AS S'N AS I CAN.

> *Are you in danger?*

> WHEN THERES LIFE THERES DANGR.

> *Who are you?*

> JUST LIKE YOU.

Mikey frowned.

> *What do you mean?*

> MIKEY, NOT IMPORTANT WHO I AM. ONLY

THING MATTERS IS WE CANT LET THEM WIN. NO
TIME TO XPLAIN NOW. BUT I HAVE A FAVOUR.

> *What?*

> HAVE A FILE THAT I NEED U 2 BROADCST.

> *Who from?*

> ONE OF THE GOOD ONES. DO WHATEVR YOU
GOT TO DO 2 GET IT OUT THERE. PROMISE ME.

> *What is it?*

> JUST PROMISE.

Mikey paused, then tapped the letters in and hit enter.

> *I promise.*

> TIMES UP. SEE YA ON FLIPSDE, MIKEY. I'LL
FIND A WAY. TRUST.

And with that the message box disappeared.

'No!' Mikey cried, desperately trying to reboot, but
the message box had crashed. The only thing left on
his screen was a rapidly downloading video file in the
right-hand corner.

He clicked on it. For a few seconds he couldn't work
out what he was seeing – a strange blue light flickering
over what looked like ice – before he suddenly made out
Michio's face on screen. And as the little Buddhabot began
to speak, Mikey's good-natured face grew grave. A thrill of
anger ran through him. Michio had helped them out so
many times – so why was he in pain, alone? Where were

the others? Mikey scanned his cell, desperately wondering how he was going to keep his promise to GERILLR.

* * *

On the bridge of the ship, a light began to flash on the control panel. Nero frowned.

'We are being hailed, ma'am.'

Önska flicked an ear. 'Captin Duchamp is here?'

'No, it's not his frequency.'

'Who den?'

'I do not know.' Nero flicked his communicator switch and a battered-up, lime-green flying banger suddenly appeared on screen, weaving and bobbing about in the powerful energy stream of their ship.

Nero activated the voice channel.

'State your business,' he said, crisply.

The screen feed now switched to the interior of the flying car – revealing Snake and Snorri jammed close together in a tatty cockpit.

Snorri looked up and waved.

'Hey, metal man, we've come for Mikey.'

Önska snorted. '*Plees.* Who is dat dirty lil man?'

Nero scanned his instruments. 'He is a pirate, ma'am.'

Snorri winked at him.

'Right you are. And I got something that might tickle yer fancy.'

Önska waggled her fat head. 'I srsly doubt that.'

'Permission to vaporise him, ma'am?' enquired Nero, his finger moving towards a red button.

'Given,' she hissed.

'Before you zap me,' continued Snorri calmly, 'you might want to take a look at what's going down at the Royale Mall of Texida—'

'Prepare to die,' said Nero, reaching for the button, but Önska held up a restraining paw.

'Wait. Lemme see.'

Live footage of a shopping mall now filled the screen and the Kat leaned forward. She vaguely remembered the Royale – she'd once had a very tasty sardine and salmon-tail smoothie there. It was one of the more upmarket malls in the state, but as she stared at the screen she could see that something was very wrong. People weren't shopping any more. People weren't smiling or sucking on NHancer drinks. At first she thought she was looking at a mob of Imps or Badlanders who'd gone on the rampage, but when she looked closer she saw this was no mob. She let out a short hiss – these were all High Net Worthers. Gone Bad. Oh, So Bad. The camera panned across the upper tier, coming to rest on two bejewelled ladies, feasting on their husbands in the entrance of a golf store, their gold bracelets jangling as they fished deep inside their life partners' skulls for gobbets of brain meat.

Önska's eyes widened in horror. 'What have you done?'

'You mean what have *you* done? You're just looking at a few of your I Am So Special customers on their zombie setting,' replied Snorri with a smirk.

'No!' hissed the Kat.

'Oh, but yes,' replied Snorri. 'We hacked your software.'

Önska's overbite gnashed into her cheek. 'Nero. Is dis really happenin?'

The droid verified the information.

'Yes. It appears as of one minute, forty-five seconds ago, an unknown hacker gained root on I Am So Special. We are not in control, ma'am.'

'Destry the hacker!' she yowled.

'Yes, but it will take a few minutes to repel them—'

'Aye it will. An' that'll be long enough fer *360 People* to get every media crew they got down there,' cut in Snake. 'Nobody will ever trust DEVA again.'

'Pah. The peeps will neva abandn us.'

'Are you sure? It's tough to come back from a secret Zombie option on all your customers.'

'I will not b blackmaild,' yowled Önska, her back arching in fury.

'Let's not call it blackmail. Let's call it . . . making a deal. We are willing to quit if you give us Mikey.'

252

'Is that whut all this is about?'

On-screen, a crew of shrieking teenage girls smashed their way through a Krispy Kreme plate-glass window and began to stagger down the mall ramp towards the car park, leaking half-chewed donuts as they went.

'They'r escaping! Stop them, Nero,' moaned the Kat.

He flung his hands up in the air. 'I cannot. You must give them the boy, ma'am. Think of the Korporation!'

'How do I knoe u will do what u say?' spat Önska, turning to face Snorri once more.

'We give yer our word. If yer hand over the lad immediately, *360 People* will never know your dirty little secret.'

Önska waved her tail. 'And what if I don't have Mikey?'

Snorri shook his head sadly. 'Then roll on the cameras.'

'Ma'am, desist. We have no option,' cried Nero.

Önska turned a furious head towards the two soldiers guarding the door.

'Bring the boi here, now.'

✝ ✝ ✝

Mikey shielded his eyes against the light as his cell door was flung open and two SPIDRs entered. One of them grabbed him by the arm.

'Come with us!' it growled.

He scrambled to his feet. 'Where are we going?'

'No questions, we ain't in the mood,' replied the other one, its middle arms twitching towards the trigger of its stun gun.

Mikey held his hands up. 'Fine, fine. I'm coming.'

But as he began to march, sandwiched between the two robot arthropods, his heart lifted. At least he was out of the cell. That was something, wasn't it?

After a few minutes he stood once more on the deck of the ship in the presence of Önska, but the Kat barely glanced his way as he entered. All her attention was on the giant air screen in the middle of the room.

'See! The boi is here,' she announced. 'We will put him on a pod, but first u must stop teh zombis.'

Mikey peered at the screen, trying to work out who she was talking to – and saw a rakish looking guy with a great mop of red curls, who turned and caught sight of him and grinned.

'Mikey, right?'

'Who are you?' asked the boy curiously.

'A buddy. Hold tight, we're getting yer out of there.' Snorri turned his attention to Önska once more. 'No deal. We stop the zombies only when Mikey's pod has left your ship.'

Önska glanced at Nero. 'Whut do u think?'

He nodded. 'Do it, quickly.'

The Kat growled deep in her throat as she ranged through millions of avoidance-strategy permutations. Why was Nero giving in so easily? Normally he was prepared to fight to the death. A new fleet of helitankers was already in the sky, loaded with the UltraRed. Nero knew the boy was vital to her plan. Something was wrong. She could feel it deep in her algorhythms . . .

'Wait! I want 2 think bout dis som more.'

Nero's head snapped round. 'We cannot delay. The Korporation has already taken a terrible hit after the Reef disaster. We will be destroyed if this gets out—'

'And *I'll* b destroyd if I let Mikey go. The UltraRed will eat us live. I am teh Korporation. If I go, we all go.'

Nero stretched himself up to his full height. 'That is not so. No one is more important than DEVA. Not even you.'

Önska lashed her tail. 'Ur insolence is Intolerble.' She mewled, reaching out for the termination button with her velvet paw of death.

'No!' cried Nero, and crossing the room in a flash, the droid struck out at her diamond cushion, sending Önska crashing to the ground.

'It is you who are terminated,' he shouted. Suddenly he turned, giving a wild salute.

'The CEO is dead. Long live the CEO.'

'Eh?' yowled Önska from the floor. 'Who r u saluting, u fool?'

A creamy soft voice cut into the room. 'Me, I belive.'

Önska twisted her head round. Directly above her appeared a glowing pink cushion, on which rode a bald Siamese kat.

'Tanny Lin!' Önska's face contorted with rage as she stared from the newcomer to Nero and back. 'Traitors!'

Tanny Lin dipped her cushion lower.

'Goodbye, me old China. Enjoy your last kitty kat breath,' she breathed, reaching for the lever of oblivion.

But then, with a bloodcurdling scream, Önska bunched up muscles that had not been bunched in over one hundred and thirty-two years of online shopping – and *leaped* at the control panel. Before Nero had time to stop her, she'd clawed her way onto the central board and, extending her graphene-tipped nails, cut through the glass of the emergency unit and slammed her paw on the sensor pad.

'Ship Self Destruct immediatly!' she screamed into the audio sensors. 'I choose death ovr def—'

Nero's heavy hand crashed down on her head. Önska slid off the control panel in a lifeless lump of fur – but as soon as her body hit the floor, a female voice came over the speaker system.

'*Thank you for your instruction. This ship will self destruct in T-minus five minutes.*'

'Override!' screamed Tanny Lin.

'Can't!' shouted Nero, staring at the panel in horror. 'No one can countermand the CEO's order.'

'But she's not in charge now. I am!'

'But she was when she made the order. It is only in the event of the CEO's death that power transfers. Trust me. It is irreversible. Our only chance is the escape pods.' Nero turned to the SPIDRs. 'Take the boy first.'

Mikey planted his feet firmly on the ground.

'No.'

Nero stared at him. 'What do you mean, no?'

Reaching inside his jacket, Mikey pulled out his tablet.

'I won't go until you broadcast this. On all Reef channels.'

Nero's face darkened. 'Move or you will die.'

'What are you doing?' shouted Snake from the cockpit.

Mikey shook his head. 'I made a promise. Play it. It's only thirty seconds.'

'Remove him by force,' spat Tanny Lin.

The SPIDRs wheeled around, extending their arms towards him. Mikey had a nanosecond in which to act. Leaping into the air, he landed a heavy punch on the base of Tanny Lin's cushion. It span wildly across the bridge before smashing against the wall, pitching the Siamese over the side. The androids stared, aghast. But before he could react, Mikey raced across the room and threw himself on top of her. For a second the pair of them rolled on the deck in a hideous, writhing, biting, scratching ball of fur and skin. Then suddenly Mikey whipped his jacket off and, smothering Tanny Lin in it, rolled her up and squeezed her tight under his arm.

'Broadcast the file or the cat gets squished,' he panted, blood dripping from his scratched nose.

Nero stared down at Mikey. One half of him *wanted* the boy to squish her. Enough of the Internet Kats. It was time for some good old-fashioned metal at the top. But he'd never survive. He'd be the droid who let the CEO die on his watch. He'd be melted down for pet-food tins.

'Miss Lin, what is your order?' he asked.

From inside the rolled up jacket came a long low moan of fury followed by a hissed, 'Do as he says.'

The female voice returned on the Tannoy system. She was a little breezier this time.

'*The ship will self destruct in T-minus four minutes. Better pack up and go, folks!*'

Nero stuck out a hand. 'All right, boy. Give me the file.'

Mikey slid his tablet across the floor.

'I won't leave till it starts playing.'

'But you have to get off the ship, it's more important than anything,' shouted Snorri from the flying car.

Mikey tightened his jaw. 'I know. So play the damn movie fast.'

Tanny Lin's sharp voice cut through the jacket. 'Pah. As if anybody cares. If anything, people will want to kill the boy for broadcasting over the new release of *Floppy Bird VI*.'

Bending over the control console, Nero's hands moved like lightning as he accessed the core of the Reef. Then he flicked a switch and suddenly Michio's face appeared on every screen, every device, every channel, every visual implant in every skull on Deva. Everybody stopped what they were doing and turned their gaze towards the synthetic's gentle face.

The video wobbled from side to side as Michio's arm trembled with the effort of holding up the camera, but when he began to speak, it was in a clear voice, and his eyes shone.

'*My friends, I wish I had time to tell you everything, but that is not possible now. All I can do now is warn you about a great danger. A poison algae called the UltraRed is heading towards you from the sea, and it will destroy you if you don't come together to fight it. DEVA has kept the truth from you,*

259

but I believe you have the right to know. The Korporation are terrified that you will panic. But I believe they have to trust you to do the right thing. Information is not the greatest danger to us. Concentration of power is.'

The video wobbled as a mortar shell exploded into the bunker wall, bringing down a huge slab of ice which rocked the table on which Michio lay. With great difficulty he again raised the screen to his face.

'What you do with my words is down to you, but I beg you to act. You cannot blame the Korporation for everything. They are only strong because you buy what they sell. In the end, it's only a passing thing, this shadow. But you must be strong. You must move. The people will always have the last word – even if someone has a very weak, quiet voice – power will collapse because of a whisper.' A sudden faint smile crossed Michio's lips. *'Destroy the UltraRed, my friends. Do it for our world, and the other. Join the rebels, now!'*

And then the screen went black.

Meanwhile, on the ship, sirens began to blare from every quarter.

'T-minus three minutes to destruction!'

Watching from the cockpit of the flying car, Snake tightened her fingers around the steering wheel as escape pods bearing Tanny Lin and Nero shot out of the ship.

'Where's Mikey?' she shouted. 'That thing is about to blow.'

Suddenly the end escape hatch opened.

'There!' cried Snorri in relief, reaching for the I Am So Special software controls as the boy's pod flew from the hull of the ship.

'Wait!'

Snake clutched his arm and Snorri looked up, his expression switching from joy to horror. A ripple of flame was streaking the length of the ship, burning brighter as it shot along the hull. Then there was a sudden terrible silence, followed almost immediately by a soft whomp – the sort of sound two pillows make when thwacked together – and then, with an almighty blast, the ship exploded into a million fragments.

'No!' screamed Snorri, shielding his eyes from the white blaze. Hurricane-strength wind slammed into the car, sending it spiralling out of control. Snake flung herself on the wheel, trying desperately to control the car in the face of the storm, but it took a full minute before she was able to wrest control again and turn the vehicle back around to face the ship. And then, for a long moment, she and Snorri stared in silence.

The ship was no more. The escape pod was no more. All that was left was a disintegrating mass of metal and plastic. Fragments of the ship still hurtled outwards, the aftershock of the explosion echoing in the sky.

Snake put her head in her hands and began to cry. *Nothing* could have survived that. Snorri put his arm around her, his face chalk white. They'd failed. The boy was dead. There was no way to ever shut the wormhole now.

And then suddenly there came a sound from over the horizon. Faint at first, it began like a whisper, before increasing in volume, becoming a kind of hissing roar. Snorri shaded his eyes and turned. On the edge of his vision, he could just make out a lashing energy current, whip-cracking across the sky. Travelling at unbelievable speed, it flashed and fizzled as it advanced towards them. Snorri gasped and rubbed his eyes, unable to comprehend what he was seeing. For, as the wave came closer and closer, there, at its very tip, he swore he could see two tiny, cube-like figures – crouched low on miniature, glowing surfboards, their faces distended with G-force as they rode the wild energy mass.

And then, small at first, but growing with massive speed, a bubble began to expand outward from the tips of their boards until it had spread across the sky, catching up the exploding debris. Soon it had encompassed every fragment of the Korporation ship, and then it began to shrink again. Snorri gasped in amazement, for, as it shrunk, the shards of metal and plastic began to flow inwards. Faster and faster, the debris moved, reforming, reattaching, clumping into larger and larger structures, until finally the ship lay whole before them again. In the cockpit, Snake's hand met his and they clutched each other tight. This was beyond weird, even for a pair of pirates who'd seen it all.

* * *

'WTF?' yowled Tanny Lin, her eyes bulging in terror as she found herself once again squished under Mikey's arm on the bridge. 'Why aren't we in the escape pod?'

Nero fell to his knees in horror. 'It's the rip, ma'am, it has dragged us back in time.'

Suddenly, in front of his furious eyes, two tiny cubes on surfboards appeared on deck, borne on a fierce swirl of energy.

'Mump, Jikey!' screamed Σëë.

The boy stared up at them.

'But I'm dead!' he shouted.

'Not mo nore!' giggled DØØ, waving his arms. 'Jump!'

'You sure?'

'Yes, yes!' they screamed.

In a daze, Mikey scrambled to his feet and caught the edge of DØØ's board with one hand.

'Atta boy!' cried DØØ, as Mikey grabbed the edge of ∑ëë's board with his other hand. 'Now let's get out of here before this ship blows!' And then, paddling furiously, the bots turned their boards and began to accelerate, sparks flying from their fingertips as they prepared to leave the ship.

Nero staggered to his feet.

'Wait! What *are* you? At least tell me that,' he howled in a most unmachine-like manner.

DØØ paused for a moment. 'The reverse of you, screwhead!'

'Yeah. We're just cubes who wanna have fun. You'd ever nundersand . . . Not in a million years!' shouted ∑ëë. And then, in a burst of tiny chuckles, they all vanished from the Nero's sight forever.

The female voice came over the Tannoy system for the last time. She had gone from breezy to soulful.

'*T-minus fifteen seconds to destruction. If there are any life forms still aboard, I'd just like to wish you luck as you enter a new dimension. Think of it as a gateway, dudes. *'

Nero and Tanny Lin stared at each other. They'd run out of time and they knew it.

'How long was I CEO for, Nero?' asked Tanny Lin in a tiny voice.

He sighed. 'Three minutes and fifty-seven seconds.

However, if one subtracts the time travel, I believe you were actually in power for fifty-seven seconds.'

Tanny Lin flattened her ears. 'Not even a minute. So, the bitch got me in the end, eh?'

He nodded morosely. 'You and me both, ma'am.'

* * *

In the cockpit of the flying car, Snake grabbed Snorri's arm as a fresh lash of energy swept towards them from the ship.

'What's going on in there?' she gasped and gripped the wheel again, trying to ride out the new wave. Despite her best efforts, the car dipped and swerved violently, before giving a final great wobble – and suddenly Mikey and the infobots were lying on the back seat in a wild sprawl.

'Go! Go! Go!' screamed DØØ.

Too amazed to argue, Snake slammed her foot down on the reverse pedal and the car screeched backwards through the air. Pressed back against the leather seats, Mikey stared at the ship through the windscreen as they pulled away.

'One hittopopamus,' counted Σëë.

'Two hittopopami,' counted DØØ.

'Three hittopopami—'

'And boom!' they shrieked, dissolving into floods of

giggles as the poor old ship blew up for the second time in a minute, buffeting the flying car high up into the air. As Snake struggled to bring the vehicle under control, Snorri turned in his seat, a huge smile plastered across his face.

'All right, Mikey?'

The boy shook his head in wonder. 'Dunno.'

The man extended his hand in greeting.

'Well, while yer making yer mind up . . . I'm Snorri the pirate.'

Mikey stared at him. 'A pirate? For real?'

'Aye, for real.' Snorri suddenly reached back and pinched the boy's ear.

'Ow!'

'Felt that, did yer?'

'Yeah.' Mikey rubbed his ear. 'What did you do that for?'

'So you'd know yer wasn't imagining me. You've been in an' out of so much madness, boy, I'm amazed yer ain't gone cuckoo.'

Mikey sighed. 'You and me both.' He leaned forward in his seat. 'All I want to do is go home, man. This place is too much.'

'Well, that's the plan, boy. Me and Snake here is goin' to give yer a ride to the mouth of the rip.'

Mikey's eyes lit up. 'Really? You know where it is?'

'Swizzleland.'

'Switzerland?'

'Aye. Yer know it?'

'As in the most boring place ever? How can that be the mouth of the wormhole?'

'Who knows? And it may not be so boring right now. I just heard there's a cheese war going on.'

'Between who?'

'The Swizzles and the Frogs.'

'The who?' Mikey blew out his cheeks. 'No. You know what? I don't want to know.' He shut his eyes. 'If you don't mind, I'm just going to lie here and relive my death experience for a bit.'

Snorri smiled. 'Knock yerself out. I'll prod yer when we get close.'

'Cheers. I just hope GERILLR makes it. He said I had to trust him.'

Snake turned in her seat. 'You *spoke* to him?'

Mikey turned his head wearily in her direction.

'Yeah, but only for a few seconds. It was him who gave me Michio's file to play.'

'So he's free then?'

'No, not yet. He said he was working on it. He said to say thanks to you guys.'

Snake's eyes sparkled. 'We did it, Snorri! We took on the Korporation.'

He held up a restraining hand. 'Not so fast, Snakey. It ain't over till the fat banker sings. Now, fly like the wind, girl.'

23

Kix stood in the valley that lay between the black hills and stared, hard, at the giant ball of cheese in front of her.

'You *sure* we got the coordinates right?'

BitZer did a little war dance on her shoulder.

'Yez. This iz Swizzleland, all right. And if you ask me that again I'z gonna get madder than a hornetz nest.'

'So why are we looking at a giant Emmental instead of the rip?'

His shoulders slumped. 'I dunno.'

He stared miserably around the valley. On another day he might have found it very pleasant, bathed as it was in a late-afternoon glow, but the whole ambience was being ruined by the gigantic bloody cheese. For the past thirty minutes he and Kix had circled the thing, clambered across it, even dug their fingers into the wax and tasted it (pleasantly nutty) but no matter what they did, the cheese remained a mile-wide round cheese and not the thing they were looking for: the mouth of a wormhole linking two parallel universes together.

Kix chewed her lip. 'GERILLR must have got confused. Or maybe we copied the coordinates down wrong?' She glanced at their car, parked on the grass behind them. 'What about taking another look from the air?'

'No. It'z here. I can feel it . . . we just izn't looking right,' replied BitZer. Staring furiously at the creamy ball, he narrowed his eyes. Suddenly he gasped. 'Hey!'

'What?'

'Half close your eyez. Then tilt your head. See?'

Rolling her head sideways, Kix squinted.

'Nope. Nothing.'

'Close 'em almost shut. Like you'z totally over the whole cheese thing. Like itz nothing to you. C'monz!'

Squeezing her eyes into tiny slits, Kix threw all her energy into a fearsomely diffident squint.

'No,' she sighed. 'It's just making my eyebrows hurt.' And then she gasped too. For suddenly, there in the heart of a gigantic Emmental cheese on the Swizzle border, she caught sight of a man in a paisley smoking jacket who was bent over a bank of instruments.

'Who's that?' she cried.

BitZer's eyes shone. 'Ha! You see it too? It'z Father Xenon Deva. I knowz that ol devil by the back of hiz handz.'

270

'But what's he doing inside the . . . cheese?' Kix reached forward, but her fingers only met the slightly sweaty surface of the rind.

'He'z not there. Not *really*.'

'Hey?'

'We'z looking at the parallel universe, girl – and not only that – at Earth, at the very moment Xenon Deva createz the wormhole. Look.'

Turning, they both trained their squinty eyes into the heart of the Emmental.

Deep in the belly of the Hadron Super Collider, Xenon Deva straightened from the bank of instruments. Genius, entrepreneur, billionaire, founder of the super-secretive DEVA Corporation, Grand Master of the Ever So Slightly Knock-Kneed Order of Californian Futurists and, of course, a few fries short of a Happy Meal – he knew his time had come. Filled with a kind of impossible calm, he moved his trembling forefinger into position over a green button that was situated on the shiny aluminium flank of the Wormhole Generator. Squeezing his eyes shut, he muttered a prayer to the God Particle. Please let it work this time.

Above him, the Super Collider magnets were now at full strength, hurtling atoms around like they were at the party at the beginning of the universe and not, in fact, on the French-Swiss border in the grip of a vicious cheese war over the branding rights to the holes in Emmental.

A shudder ran through the concrete walls of his bunker. Xenon Deva took a deep breath, jabbed the green button and – WHOOOOSH – a shining streak of dancing negative atoms materialised out of thin air and spiralled up out of the Collider into the sky. He stared at his instruments in amazement. Yes! At last! He'd done it! He'd created a bridge to a parallel Earth! A Techno-Utopia where humanity could start again. He jammed his fists on his hips, preparing himself for a burst of wild Mad-Scientist Laughter. Boy, he deserved it.

'Stop!' yelled Kix, hammering on the cheese rind from the edge of the meadow. Beside her, BitZer hurled himself at the wax, but to no avail. They were on the wrong side, helpless viewers at the most ridiculous man-made disaster of all time. And then Kix suddenly realised that they weren't alone. Someone was behind her, addressing her in a dry, official voice.

'Excuse me, Fräulein . . .'

She whirled around to see a thin, suited man in a little hairnet flanked by a line of burly guards with zapper guns.

She stared at him in amazement before nudging BitZer. 'We've got company.'

The hairnetted man stared at her curiously before

clearing his throat with a little cough.

'Ahem, wilkommen. I wonder if perhaps you are representatives from the Maison du Gruyère factory?'

Kix stared at him blankly. 'Pardon?'

'The Maison du Gruyère factory. Representatives. You?' the dry man repeated.

'No-o, I don't think so,' replied Kix, wondering if the fromage had somehow pushed her over the edge of reason.

The man gave a little bow. 'Of course not. Forgive me.' He pursed his lips, considering. 'Then maybe you are of the Schabziger people?'

'Shab – zigga –?' stuttered Kix. She poked BitZer with her finger. 'You can see this man too, right?'

BitZer waggled his head. 'Unfortunately, yez.'

'So, I've not gone mad then?'

'Not unless I haz too.'

'Well, have you?'

He waggled his head some more.

'Hard to know for sure.'

Kix jerked her thumb towards the man, who was now growing visibly tetchy.

'Let's say we haven't gone mad. In which case, what's he talking about?'

'Cheeze,' hissed BitZer.

'That is so!' The man steepled his fingers severely. 'Fräulein, you are standing in a war zone. I really must insist on knowing which cheese house you are from.'

Kix summoned up a smile. 'Of course, yes. *We* are from the – ah . . .' she glanced desperately at BitZer who was rapidly pulling up information.

He looked up, triumphant. 'We are from the . . . Tomme de Savoie region.'

Kix smiled in relief. 'Yes, that's us!'

And then she stopped smiling as she saw the effect that BitZer's words had on the group. The man gave a great cry of rage, and the guards instantly took out their guns and pointed them menacingly in their faces.

'You. Are. From. The. *Frog.* Side?' gasped the man.

'What have you done?' Kix hissed in BitZer's ear.

'Not sure . . .' whispered Bitzer.

'Fix it. Quick.'

Turning to the man, she spread her hands. 'Of course, we are not from the Frog side. We are Swizzles through and through.' She poked BitZer in the ribs. 'Tell these gentlemen what cheese house we're *really* from.'

'We are . . .' began BitZer desperately, 'from the Appenzell region in Swizzleland. And we bring the *Appenzeller* – a robust cheese that's pungent in aroma and—'

'Liar!' roared the official. 'You are spies! Guards, arrest them immediately.'

'Get offz!' cried BitZer, bravely backing into Kix's scarf as the men closed in.

'You don't understand – we're trying to save you!' shouted Kix as the nearest guard laid his meaty paw on her shoulder.

The little man drew himself up to his full height. 'Lies. We do not need saving. The holes in Emmental will soon be ours, all ours. Without any help from you.' He flicked a glance at the guards.

'Take them away.'

BitZer and Kix exchanged despairing looks, but they had no choice but to fall in line as the guards surrounded them – and in seconds they found themselves being marched away from the Emmental towards a hut at the base of a wooded slope. As she walked, Kix clenched her fists in impotent rage. She'd always known that human civilisation couldn't last, but she'd imagined the species checking out with more style than this. Like from a deadly virus. Or in a global war. Or from a meteor storm, at the very least. But never in her wildest dreams did she imagine that fourteen billion people on two different planets were going to die because of a bunch of insane dairy-product *bureaucrats*.

And then suddenly, out of the sky there came a heavy rumbling sound, followed by an immense gust of wind that knocked them all flat to the ground. Fighting against the terrible downward force, Kix managed to lift her head a few centimetres. Around her, the guards were crawling towards the safety of the woods, but Kix gripped the turf, flipped herself over on her back and looked upwards – at the gigantic helitanker bearing down on her from above. Her jaw dropped.

'What's that doing here?'

'DEVA. They must've found out where we iz!' screamed BitZer.

'No! We've got to stop—'

But the rest of Kix's words were drowned out as the tanker doors slid open and a vast sluice of UltraRed plummeted directly onto the cheese wheel. The effect was electrifying – like throwing gasoline on a smouldering fire. A great arc of flaming atoms appeared and suddenly the mouth of the wormhole was visible as it roared into life.

As soon as it had dropped its load, the helitanker wheeled away as fast as it had come, and in moments, it was a dot on the horizon.

Kix dragged herself to her knees.

'No, no,' she groaned.

'Holdz your horsez, girlie! Look!' BitZer pointed his bendy finger towards the horizon. She turned to see a lime-green flying car barrelling over the edge of the mountains in a haze of dirty smoke. Moving towards them at crazy speed, it took only a few moments for it to come screeching to a burning, skidding halt on the grass alongside them.

BitZer jumped up, hopefully.

'Mikey?'

The car door popped open in a hiss of dirty smoke and Mikey, Snorri and Snake scrambled out.

'Too late! They've dumped the UltraRed in the wormhole!' wailed Kix.

The others turned to look. Deva and the Emmental had now entirely disappeared. All that was left was a roaring vat of negative atomic cheese.

'Are you ready?' shouted Kix.

Mikey backed away, his face pale with terror.

'I'm not going in there!' he shouted.

BitZer jumped onto his shoulder. 'But you *haz* to.'

Mikey whirled his arms around. 'Why me? I don't see anyone else around here jumping into a boiling fondue.'

Snorri sucked his teeth. 'Boy's got a point.'

Kix grabbed him by the shoulder. 'You know why.

I'd go instead of you if I could, Mikey, but I can't. I –
I'm sorry.'

He laughed wildly. 'You're *sorry*? I'll remember that
when the skin is melting off my face like old mozzarella.'

She clutched his hand. 'Mikey. You've got to trust it.
The rip got you here and it'll take you back too.'

'Why?'

'Because you're *you*, dude. The universe must've picked
you for a reason. If you can't make it, no one can.'

Mikey stared at her in amazement. 'Are you being
nice to me for real or just nice so I'll get in the mac 'n
cheese?'

'For real.' She laughed, punching him on the arm.
'You've kind of grown on me, Monkey boy.'

Mikey turned and gazed at the churning rip. Then he
took a deep breath. 'All right, I'll do it. But only if GERILLR
comes.' He craned his neck upwards. 'Where is he? He
said he'd be here.'

'Then we'z gotta truzt him. He'z done everything else
he promised,' replied BitZer softly.

In silence, they all turned their eyes to the sky, while
beneath them the ground shuddered and groaned. On
the far side of the meadow, a great rent suddenly started
to open the earth up.

'He's got to come soon or it'll be too late. This thing

is going to blow,' whispered Snorri.

'What's that?' hissed Snake, pointing eastwards, to where a blinding jag of light flashed across the sky. A clap of thunder that reverberated across the valley, bouncing from crag to crag, followed it. And then suddenly a dazzling star appeared over the horizon, hurtling in a long, blazing arc towards them.

'It's him!' screamed Kix. The brilliant thing drew closer and closer until, directly overhead, it slowed, almost seeming to hang in the sky above them, and for a brief moment they were able to catch a glimpse of it. A shining, golden ape – or was it something more humanlike? For a second the body rotated, glinting in the sunlight, before plunging down into the heart of the wormhole – and as it disappeared, there was a roar and a great confusion of noise before suddenly the flame died away and a terrible silence fell across the valley.

'Now, Mikey!' whispered Kix, putting her hand on his shoulder.

'Aye, boy. Now or never,' breathed Snorri.

Mikey took a deep breath. And then, calling up all his courage, he forced himself to walk towards the mouth of the rip. He had to do it. For Earth. For Deva. For his fellow man. He stopped walking, remembering he didn't give a rat's arse for his fellow man and he turned and looked back at his friends. Their faces were drawn with terrible tension, as if it was them about to stride into the cheeseball of hell, not him. But it wasn't them. It was him. He felt a lick of anger. He was such a fool for agreeing to this – and then he felt a tickle on his neck, and glancing down, he saw Σëë and DØØ standing on his shoulder.

'You're our mero, Hikey!' whispered Σëë, staring up into his face.

'Treally, ruly,' added DØØ, standing on his tiptoes to kiss him on the nose.

Mikey shook his head. 'I'm nobody's hero, dudes. I – I don't want to do it.'

Σëë nodded, his tiny eyes full of tiny tears. 'But you're going to anyway. That's why you're our boy.'

'And 'sides . . . the rip won't dare hurt you, you're Mikey Malone.'

Mikey looked DØØ straight in the eye.

'You sure?'

The cube nodded solemnly. 'Dost mefinately.'

The infobots looked so serious that Mikey burst out laughing, and bending down, he gently put them on the grass.

'Thanks for everything, guys.'

'It was a fot of lun, Mikey,' they giggled, bowing in unison.

And with that, Mikey turned back to the rip – and sticking out his chest, he stepped into the ring of dancing atoms and vanished from sight.

Kix gasped as a violent hiss shot out of the wormhole, like steam escaping a giant pressure cooker. The ground underneath her began to collapse as if huge engines had ignited underground. She staggered sideways. She could hear Snorri calling her name, but she wasn't able to move.

Suddenly she felt his arms around her.

'Come on!' he cried, dragging her towards the woods.

And then, with an almighty bang, the rip exploded into the sky – and from its heart came a drumming rumble, a roar, and then, with a final flash of wild energy that shook the whole valley, it disappeared.

* * *

Mikey fell. Spiralling down, down, down into the continuum, he plunged through impossible curves and great yawning chasms of space and time. It was too much for his mind to take. Black stars began to flicker across his vision but before he lost consciousness, he stiffened, opening his eyes wide in horror. For he suddenly heard a voice, an *unmistakable* voice that echoed across the void, crying, 'IDIOT BUMHOLE!'

His heart spasmed in rage. But before he could turn to

look for Ubu, everything went black. Really black this time. Blacker than a yard down a bear's throat. Blackety black black. And then, with one last lashing curve, the wormhole flung him free.

24

Mikey opened his eyes. He was lying on his bedroom floor and Caitlin was standing just a metre or so away in the doorway, in the exact same spot where he'd left her. He shook his head in amazement. He'd made it. Joy bubbled up in his heart and, rolling himself into a sitting position, he grinned.

'Hey, what's up, Cat?' he cried.

She stared back at him with eyes wide open.

'What's going on?' she stammered.

Mikey frowned. This wasn't exactly the welcome he'd been looking for.

'I'm back,' he answered, trying to keep his voice light.

'But you're not gone . . . You're . . .' she pointed with a trembling hand towards the corridor behind her, 'over there.'

From the corner of his eye, Mikey caught a glimpse of someone moving towards him along the passageway.

Someone with the same mad hair . . . someone wearing the same T-shirt as him . . .

'What's going on?' he shouted thickly. He felt faint and sick all of a sudden, like he'd been punched in the guts. And then, slowly, with a heavy sense of dread, he forced himself to turn and look at himself, as he stood in the bedroom doorway, staring back at him with terrified eyes. No! This could only mean one thing . . . that the rip was still open and he was in two parallel universes at once.

'What?' yelled both Mikeys simultaneously.

A deadly cold poured into Mikey's body and he fell, twitching to the ground. And then it hit him. He *knew* what had happened. Ubu had stayed inside the wormhole, preventing it from being shut. The whole plan had been ruined by a single, psychotic parrot. Mikey shut his eyes in horror.

The deadly UltraRed was now somewhere on Earth.

The universe still had an extra seven billion Kalifornians it never asked for.

But worst of all, now there were two of him and only one Caitlin.

He couldn't win, whatever he did.

Mikey began to claw his way towards the window. He had to get as far away as he could from his double. He didn't know what he was going to do, but he knew that he *had* to do something. The future of Deva and Earth hung in the balance – and he was the only one who knew what danger they were in.

Except for one other person . . . but his unconscious body lay on the floor of cubicle 20280 in the Wei Han Industrial Complex in China. And who knew if GERILLR would ever wake again?

Acknowledgements

I'd just like to thank a few people without whom this book would never have been finished.

First, my incomparable editor, Rachel Wade, who championed the early madness of this novel. Also, Emma Goldhawk, who has nurtured it through the later stages. Anne McNeil, for her fine, gimlet-eyed style, and everyone at Hachette for their fantastic support.

Also, anyone who has had to listen to me ramble on about parallel universes.

And robots.

And the future of the world.

Oh, and of course, a big thank you to my agent, Veronique Baxter, for always being in my corner. It really means a lot.

P.S. All life forms portrayed within the parallel universe of this book are fictitious and any resemblance to humanoids living or dead is purely coincidental and hopefully amusing.

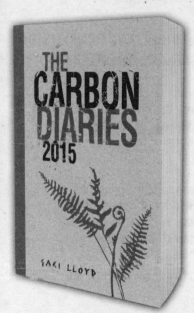

 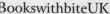

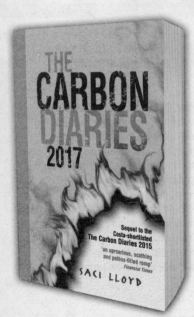

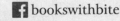

EVERYTHING STARTS RIGHT HERE RIGHT NOW
MOMENTUM

SACI LLOYD

London, the near future. Energy wars are flaring across the globe - oil prices have gone crazy, regular power cuts are a daily occurrence. The cruel Kossak soldiers prowl the streets, keeping the Outsiders - the poor, the disenfranchised - in check. Hunter is a Citizen: one of the privileged of society, but with his passion for free running and his rebel friend Leo he cannot help but be fascinated by the Outsiders. So when he meets Outsider Uma, he is quickly drawn into their world - and into an electrifying and dangerous race to protect everything they hold dear.

A hugely exciting dystopian thriller from the immensely talented Costa-shortlisted author of The Carbon Diaries, Saci Lloyd.

'From its breathtaking opening ... an action-packed thriller with a warm heart' – The Guardian

www.hodderchildrens.co.uk

Hodder
Children's
Books

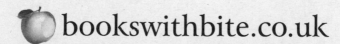